3.95 Doldy. 33⅓%

A Candle in the Sun

By the Same Author

A CANDLE
IN THE SUN

Marguerite Steen

DOUBLEDAY & COMPANY, INC.

GARDEN CITY, NEW YORK

1964

All of the characters in this book are fictitious, and any resemblance to actual persons, living or dead, is purely coincidental.

"To enlarge or illustrate this power and effect of love is to set a candle in the sun."
Robert Burton, *The Anatomy of Melancholy*

A Candle in the Sun

Chapter One

The sky was black with incipient snow. Fog knitted itself into the hoary tangle of hornbeams and at mid-day rosy lights glowed in windows set back in frost-bound plantations. The old hired Chevrolet jolted over iron-hard ruts or skidded on sheets of ice. There were dead birds and, when they came in sight of the Sound, floes racing down the water which, instead of warming, communicated an even more penetrating chill to the land.

A couple of miles from Idlewild, George Ginever looked at his watch and knew they were not going to make it. Two days to Christmas, and all the flights overloaded; grace and favour, and a fortuitous acquaintance with one of the airline chiefs, alone had procured him a reservation when, at the last moment, they made up their minds that he must get home for Christmas.

Used to the speed of Luce's Thunderbird, he had miscalculated the time to the airport; or, rather, he had not allowed for the caution of the elderly driver—aimed less at mutual safety than at the preservation of his deplorable vehicle. Easing it over every hummock, pausing at the little crossroads, with not a thing in sight, to poke his withered turtle-head in every direction—long before they reached the parkway he had Ginever taut with irritation.

1

"Looks like we wuz going to be a mite late," he murmured, crashing from second to first and jerking his passenger towards the dashboard as he let the clutch in with a bang.

"How about pulling in and taking a rest?" suggested Ginever, drawing upon himself a look of surly suspicion, which he told himself he had earned. It was one of his principles, never to employ sarcasm on dependents—though this character hardly rated the description, and no doubt would have resented it with all the force of his New England spirit.

"Do you want we turn round right now, mister?" he snarled, but hope gleamed in the corner of his eye, and Ginever realised that he was honestly scared of the treacherous surface, the poor visibility, and the screaming traffic they were approaching.

"No, carry on," he muttered. Having got so far, the practical thing was to go on to the airport, find out if there happened to be any cancellations on later flights, and if there was nothing, make back for Oyster Bay—having first given Luce a warning ring. It would be the worst sort of anti-climax, to get back and find the place locked up, and Luce gone out some place, to avoid her loneliness.

He made himself relax, and tried to keep his mind off the hope he was tempted to indulge: that they might after all have the Christmas they had both longed for, and resigned because they agreed they owed it to Flavia. It could be the last Christmas the Ginevers, father and daughter, would have together for a long time; there was no reason to suppose that his wife would be generous if the divorce went through.

He cursed his refusal to let Luce drive him to the airport, and the growing certainty that he had missed the plane. When you have made up your mind to a distasteful course of action, postponement is worse than the action itself.

"You're quite sure you want a divorce?"
Luce's hands on his shoulders, her honest eyes nearly on a

2

level with his own, commanded the truth. He loved those eyes—much too large for her ashen little face, deep grey, humorously tilted at the outer corners, even in her moments of utmost seriousness. She was not in the least beautiful—perhaps he was tired of beauty; she was too tall, too thin. The voice that came out of her big, generous mouth was an absurd baritone—almost as deep as his own. Cut off the springing copper hair that brushed her shoulders, flatten her small, tip-tilted breasts, and she could have passed for a jaded youth. Yet she was the most tender and feminine thing that had come in George Ginever's way since—since when? He did not care to think.

Knowing it was not the moment for loverly protestations, he assured her simply that it was so.

"Have you ever felt that way before?"

"No."

"Not for anybody?"

"Not for anybody."

"Why not?" she persisted; her fingers, like strips of steel, bit into his shoulder blades.

He sought for the answer, and found it after a long silence.

"I imagine—because it wasn't worth while."

"God." She chuckled in her throat. "You must have been awful to your women."

He thought that over, and disagreed. He could have retorted that some of them had been "awful" to him. At the same time, it occurred to him that he had perhaps been over-candid with Luce in regard to his extra-marital career. And yet—he wondered—how could he regret the impulse of complete honesty that had followed their coming together? Or was it honesty? Was it a form of insurance against Luce's finding out things he would have preferred to conceal?—his personal record of infidelity, details unimportant (they had not gone into those) but adding up to an unpleasant total?

She gurgled when he blundered something of this out to

3

her, and he realised he was sounding ridiculous—like one of
the Romney-Lustgarten columns in the *Sunday Express:*
"Should one tell?"

They settled on the long couch in front of the big log fire;
the black winter crowded against the windows and was re-
pelled by the inner glow; Luce's old spaniel nuzzled into the
bearskin rug and made sweet sleep-sounds.

"Why didn't Blythe divorce you? I would have."

"She didn't care enough. Neither did I."

"Well, is she likely to care this time?"

"Blythe's a very nice person." He spoke carefully. "Basically, we don't like each other. But she understands me—up
to a point. Which is why, so far, the question of divorce hasn't
arisen. I could have been in a hell of a mess, by now, if
Blythe had divorced me. She's been very generous. She hasn't
had a good time, over these last years."

"And she hasn't wanted a life of her own?"

"Apparently not. She's not 'wifely'—if that's the word. She's
got her home, and plenty of interests—a few of which we
share. But, as I've explained, she isn't in any sense of the
word dependent on me. The house belongs to her, and she's
got ample means of her own. She's what I suppose you'd call
self-sufficient. She isn't emotional, and she's lost her interest
in sex; it wasn't ever very strong."

"But—" Puzzled, Luce knitted her brows. "I don't see—at
that rate—why she didn't let you go."

He shrugged his shoulders.

"I didn't want to be 'let go,' and Blythe knew it; that's part
of the answer. The other part is, the existing position was
convenient for both of us. I supplied something she wanted.
She liked having me there for public occasions; she liked first
nights and film premiers and dinners and luncheons and public platforms and interviews and sessions with press photographers and all the jazz. It sounds childish: but there is
that childish side to Blythe. It's one of the things I've always

4

found rather touching and—well, in a way lovable about her. It's so out of key with her general character. I could at least give her that, in return for all she gave me. Which wasn't a little."

"So," said Luce, after a long pause, "it all depends on Blythe." She saw his face and covered his hand quickly with her own. "I didn't mean that. It depends on us: on you and me. There's no hurry, you know," she reminded him gently.

"For me, there's hurry."

After sixteen years of an arid marriage—admitted as such on both sides—how, he asked himself, could there not be hurry? He was sharply aware of his age; when you are into your forties you want to make the most of summer, before accepting the autumn. He wanted to bring Luce all the richness of his prime, the urgence, the violence, the ripeness, the best of himself. He wanted all the years ahead to belong unconditionally to Luce; to have her by his side in success or failure; if any honours came his way to share them with her. This he tried haltingly to tell her: keeping his vocabulary, as far as he could, quiet, dispassionate and reasonable.

"What a fuss you make about age," said Luce—twelve years younger than he. "Don't fuss so, darling. There's plenty of time. Blythe's got to get used to the idea. Considering everything"—she gave her quiet laugh—"she can't be blamed if she doesn't take it in at first."

She got up to throw more logs on the fire, and remained squatting on her heels, staring at the flames. He thought, Oh God, we've only got a few more hours! and reached to pull her back against his knees.

"How long is it since things went wrong—really wrong—between you?" she asked.

He could have answered that they had never been really right, but it did not seem necessary to make himself out a bigger fool than he was, even to Luce.

"A very long time; soon after Flavia was born."

5

"And she's fifteen, isn't she? What's she going to make of this?"

"I haven't the least idea. That's another of the things I've got to find out."

"Do you think she'll be upset?"

He shrugged his shoulders.

"She may be—a little; but she's got a lot of common-sense. No, I don't think she will make heavy weather of it, when she has taken it in."

"Is that what you think, or what you want to think?" persisted Luce. He laughed a little.

"She's an intelligent kid; she's grown up with the situation, and it must more or less have sunk in by now, although we've gone to a good deal of trouble not to force it on her—I mean, by airing our differences in front of her, or any of that kind of thing. I don't remember ever criticising her mother to her, and I should imagine Blythe has been loyal in that way to me; it would be part of her concept of good manners!"

"Yes, she had wonderful manners," murmured Luce. "She's the kind of person you could know for twenty years without getting any idea of whether she liked you or not."

"That's grown on her. It's difficult to be unreserved if you are made to feel your confidences are unappreciated. I'd feel worse about Blythe if she hadn't an outlet in Flavia."

"Are they very devoted to each other?"

"They used to be. Flavia's cooled off a little— No," he corrected himself. "That's not fair. She's growing up; she's got an independent nature and probably there's some degree of sex antagonism. Or she may find Blythe's attitude a little oppressive."

"So she's swung towards you?" hazarded Luce.

"Well, yes, I suppose that describes it."

"What are you being sheepish about?" asked Luce, with her beautiful, wide grin. "It's natural for a girl to swing towards her father, and anyhow you're crazy about Flavia."

6

"I want to see her before she goes off to her boarding school."

"Yes, of course. That's important," said Luce seriously. "But," she begged, "don't *rush* anything. Even when you and Blythe have come to an—an understanding, don't fling it at Flavia. Promise me, will you? I know that generation's supposed to take divorce in its stride, but I've got a hunch about this. Please let's hurt people as little as possible! I've got a superstitious thing about hurting. I wonder—" her voice trailed away.

"What do you wonder?"

"If it would help if I came over to Europe. My brother-in-law's got an apartment in Passy, and it's ages since I promised to visit them. It might ease matters a little, if Flavia and I could meet before you told her about us."

This struck him as so admirable an idea that he asked her how soon she could come.

"Well—not immediately." She sounded startled at being taken so promptly at her word.

"For New Year's?"

"Now, now!"

He took her by the nape of her thin neck and screwed her head round towards him.

"Stop acting prissy and answer my question."

"Listen: when you get home you'll think of all sorts of things we've not had time to consider. You've got all your work and your business to straighten out. You've got to make adjustments with Flavia—that'll take time—and settle things with Blythe—"

"And suppose Blythe refuses to 'settle'?"

"Is she likely—?"

"Haven't I told you Blythe's incalculable?" He pulled her up beside him and held her. "Let's face everything, shall we? Supposing Blythe won't divorce me: what then?"

7

"Meaning, will I continue to be your mistress, and live with you." Her voice was deadly calm.

"Meaning, do you love me enough to accept the only sort of position I'd be able to offer you."

"Do you want me to accept it?" she asked quietly.

He dropped his head on her hands, realising, for the first time, the full meaning of his love for Luce; certainly the first truly unselfish love he had ever known. The modern idea was, of course, that it did not matter if people were married or not; the slapdash social pattern took in casual couples, accepted with indifference wives or mistresses. But there were still certain acceptances, certain privileges to which the unmarried wife could not aspire. Whether or not she cared about them, he would resent it if they were not offered to Luce; he would bitterly resent Blythe's continued monopoly of such petty kudos as attached to the wife of George Ginever on public occasions. In a position like his, there were considerations beyond the gratification of living with and sleeping with the woman you loved. And he realised he loved Luce too much to offer that equivocal place, which would mean, for her, a sacrifice of status he had no right to demand.

"Let's not worry for the present," she was saying, into his silence. "Let's just pretend it's going to be all right. I'll come over to Paris as soon as I can—"

"How soon's that?" he demanded.

"Look," she said, in her deep voice. "You've got to be free for a while: free, and apart, to consider things we've had no time to discuss; to make decisions my being around can only confuse. This isn't just you and me; it concerns other people as well."

"I gave up what you're pleased to call my 'freedom' five nights ago; do you remember?" He felt a shiver run through her. "I made it over to you—for what it's worth. Is the responsibility too much?" He waited, and as she made no reply,

8

told her, "You know—you ought to know—I have no longer any life apart from you."

This conversation took place on the night before his departure. They rang Luce's sister in Paris, and she was on the point of taking off for a holiday in the Canaries; Paris was "*infecte*" and terribly expensive; the "*plastiques*" were getting on everybody's nerves—she had sent the children and their nanny away to their grandparents' place in Dordogne. "Honey, it's just too bad; after all these years do you have to pick this moment?" "No, we can fix it later. I just happened to feel like taking a trip to Paris.— So that's out," said Luce.

"You know, there are some quite goodish hotels in Paris," he told her seriously. She grinned.

"You're telling me. But I'd like, just for a while, to keep in with Belle-mère. She'd think it curious if I went to Paris, *not* to stay with Carola. She's got the idea that a young widow's got to be protected! I had a hell of a time over going back to the theatre; in the end I had to tell her I'd go crazy or become an alcoholic if I'd nothing to do but sit around in a deep blue dream about The Past."

"But—lord save us—she didn't expect you to dedicate your life to a ghost?"

"Not exactly. But she's possessive—and she's very fond of me; and by God, I owe her plenty! Vic left his affairs in a mess, and I have this cottage on—what do you call it?—a peppercorn rent."

"But she must realise you've got some sort of future."

"Sure," nodded Luce. "She'd like to control it, that's all. I think she takes it for granted I'll marry again, someday, but there's got to be 'the decent interval,' and she's got to have a say over the husband.— No, of course I don't accept it," she said, in answer to his impatient exclamation. "What do you take me for?— But I'm sorry for her; underneath all that shiny, social stuff there's a very sad old woman. She'd pinned everything on Vic; his death was a bigger shock to her than it was

9

to me. She took to her clubs and her psychiatrists and her masseurs and her fortune-tellers as I took to the theatre. So we understand each other. So I can't let her down over all this Christmas and New Year's racket, when she counts on me to carry the ball."

"What I don't get," said Ginever, knowing Luce's mother-in-law, "is the way you look on her as old. She's been extremely kind to me, but she wears me down!"

"She wears everybody down—me too. She's sixty—and that's not old in these days. But at the pace Belle-mère's lived her life it makes her virtually a centenarian. She's still living a dream-life in her roaring forties, but all crazy-mixed-up with the conventions of her youth." Luce laughed gently. "It makes it difficult for people—younger people—to have patience with her; Vic never had. She idolised him in the most sickening fashion, and it almost made him hate her. Since he was killed I've tried to make up to her for all he inflicted on her—and I can't withdraw that suddenly.

"Let's take it we've both got commitments: you to Blythe and Flavia, me to Belle-mère. If we play it easily, it'll work out."

"Littlejohn's still nagging about taking the play to London," he told her presently.

"Yeah, I know."

"Every London manager turned it down. Now it seems they think it's got a better chance there than it's had in New York."

"By the time it closes here you'll have had an eight months' run; not bad for Broadway."

"If it comes to town," he blundered, "would you like to take over Aurelia?"—the part she had been understudying.

"No," said Luce. He laughed.

"You hate the play, don't you?"— She had given up her understudy a few weeks earlier; she was lucky, she did not have to earn her living in the theatre.

"You said the other day, if the play goes to London, it means a re-write."

"Only of a couple of scenes and a bit of dialogue. With luck, a fortnight's work."

"Look, you aren't a playwright. You hate the theatre as much as I do. You happened, by accident, to write a play—in collaboration with Pete Marrotti. Two big names got it a run on Broadway; if the Webbs hadn't taken a fancy to it, you know it wouldn't have run a week," said Luce tenderly. "If Leo and Cath took a couple of pages out of the telephone directory and chose to put them on the stage, they'd get away with it; they did very well with that piece of Marrotti's, *Mouse in Space*—do you remember?"

"Thanks for the memory," said Ginever.

"But the Webbs aren't bringing it to London; she's got something by Faulkner in her head, and a guy called I forget what is working on it for her. You and Marrotti were a fill-in between their flop in the Spring and this notion of Cath's."

"And Bill Littlejohn thinks it will go in London." He stuck to his point.

"I wouldn't know. But—look: the theatre is ruinous to people not of the theatre. You've done no real work this fall, because you've been tied up with Cath and Leo. Belle-mère's been pushing you around—"

"No," he corrected her. "She's been pretty good about that."

"Anyhow," said Luce, "you must get away from this absurd play! And forget about this novel—and get yourself in the mood for the Big Book. Like a surprise? Okay. I'm learning Spanish. I am! I didn't tell you, because I thought I mightn't make it; I never was particularly good at languages. But it's surprisingly easy. I go to classes twice a week and I've got a Spanish girl who reads with me whenever we've got time: she's got a job at the Embassy. We spend more time reading

11

maps than reading Spanish literature! She's a madrileña—one of the real moderns; she hadn't even heard of Gracián—well, yes, she'd heard of him, like our kids have heard of Shakespeare. He meant nothing to her. But she's helped me work out a travel route—I'll show it you.

"Honey." She held both his hands. "Get back to Europe. Get away from all this *malilla*—there: you see I've learnt a real Spanish word!—*malilla* of the theatre and the sort of fiction you don't want to write; you know you don't want to."

"Sounds as if you can't wait to get shut of me!"

"Perhaps," she said soberly, "I can't wait to get rid of this character that flits round the networks and the women's clubs and the cocktails parties; this character that sometimes gets between me and George Ginever."

"Dammit, I hate the jazz as much as you do; you know that. And, as I've told you, I've got to earn a living." He paused. "There're some things we haven't got down to—"

"Let's not, for the present," she interrupted. "Those can come later. First things first. And first's this Gracián book of yours. Get your mind off me for a while and get back into the mood of your Jesuits and your seventeenth-century philosophers—"

"You ask too much."

"I shall always ask much!" she flashed at him.

"Do you know, apart from my secretary, Ann Maxton, you're the first person I've ever talked to about my Gracián?"

"All right; then send me that translation by that friend you told me about. If we have to wait— What was it you said the other night: something about 'all-embracing patience'?" she interrupted herself.

" 'Hombre de espera'—yes. 'To know how to wait is the sign of a great heart endowed with an all-embracing patience.' " He shook his head. "Part of old Baltasar's doctrine of perfection.

"Hard to live up to: like the rest of his Oracles."

"Well, we could try. Send me the book, and let me feel we are together in your work . . ."

It was anti-climax, on reaching the airport forty minutes after the plane was due out, to be told there was a delay on the London flight. How long? A couple of hours, probably. He checked in his small amount of baggage and put in a call to Oyster Bay.

Her voice was deeper and rougher than usual, and he guessed she had been weeping.

"For crying out loud! I've been picturing you up in the sun for the last hour. How long a delay do you say? Two hours? That means three or four. Hold it: I'm coming."

"No, you're not." He had refused to let her drive him to Idlewild for two reasons: first that, like most habitual travellers, he loathed being "seen off"—the petering out of intelligent conversation into a trickle of clichés, one ear cocked for the public announcements, emotional tension giving way to the longing only to be gone. Farewells at railway termini were not so bad; you could time the moment of departure with a reasonable degree of certainty. But the imponderables of long-distance take-offs by air had yet to be solved; science had not discovered the answers.

There was another good reason for not letting Luce take him to Idlewild. As part-author of a play still running on Broadway, novelist, lecturer, and interviewee on TV, his face was well enough known to catch the attention of some roving cameraman with film to use up. A pressman short of material for his column might take a chance.

It was George Ginever's misfortune to be photogenic. Even in his twenties, photographers, professional and amateur, had seen the publicity value in that curiously aged, yet ageless face, thin, lined, puffy under the eyes, the delicate yellowish skin drawn loosely over the impeccable bone structure. On any pub-

13

lic occasion, whoever missed the camera's eye it was never Ginever—though he might be the most insignificant person present. It had started at Oxford; in Eights week or at Commem balls, the insignificant undergraduate was invariably featured, with some dazzling débutante, in the glossies. Who was George Ginever? Nobody knew; but he made too good a picture to be left out. The Adonis vogue was out. A simple youth, socially clumsy (though a good dancer), Ginever did not even register the names of most of the young women with whom he had a dance or two, with whom, inevitably, he was photographed. Too shy to flirt, their advances usually alarmed him. And eventually he bored them, because his social achievements did not bear out the promise of his unusually sophisticated looks.

At the age of twenty, he looked thirty; at forty, he could have been sixty, or a dissipated eighteen. A mood, an angle of lighting, could translate him to either. He measured a fraction over six feet, but reduced it by his "scholar's stoop," which had nothing whatever to do with scholarship, but was the result of an accident on the playing fields while he was still at school. Torn muscles and an unsuccessful piece of surgery set up the habit of slightly bending to relieve tension on the damaged bit of anatomy—which, when the war came along, disqualified him for active service.

Photographs of himself and Luce, flashed to the English papers with some suggestive caption, would not sweeten the situation when he got home. Blythe might smile her wry, indifferent smile at just one more of those things she had brushed off over the years. But this was not one of those things. It was mainly for this reason that he refused Luce's offer of transport and hired the old Chevvy driven by her handyman.

He wanted to carry away intact the memory of their last night. And the hour after breakfast on Luce's narrow four-poster with its arched tester and dimity ruffles. And the exquisite fretwork of frosted branches outside the windows. And Luce standing on the frosted porch, waving him off, the bleak light on her thin face, one beautiful thin hand thrust into the pocket of her English tweed slacks, the broad, artificial smile masking her inner grief. Luce, his laughing companion, his loved one, with whom he wanted to share everything, good times and bad, success and failure. The one who, after all the empty years, was re-shaping the pattern of his life, brushing off its tawdry accretions. All of his will was now bent to making the new pattern, the Luce-pattern, permanent.

The daylight faded, the hours stretched out. He put in another call—it was only prolonging the agony, but the next time he heard her voice would be across the void of the Atlantic. This time there was no reply. He went to the bar and got himself a drink. And then another. Then a man with whom he had got into conversation insisted on buying him another, and by that time there were four or five, all cursing the air lines, and Ginever bought a round . . .

She came, swooping like a bird, through the disgruntled, bored, and blasphemous crowd. Speechless and incredulous, he watched her approach; he was unable even to speak her name. She lifted her thin, grey face to his, and as their lips touched the speaker boomed over their heads. Luce said calmly:

"There: that's your flight. Goodnight, darling."

"For God's sake," he mumbled, "take it easy." Luce drove like an inspired maniac; he had a fuddled vision of the parkway, and the iced-up lanes. She laughed.

"Sure; it's pure glass. That's why I'm so late. Happy landing. Call me tomorrow."

He stumbled across the tarmac. The snow had started to fall and danced against the lights. He tripped on the gangway and a steward caught his arm and steered him into a seat. Automatically he obeyed the injunction to fasten the safety belt. As the plane trundled down the runway, he thought of

Luce in her Thunderbird, making back through the snow to her empty house. The last moments, the last touch of their flesh, was a crazy dream.

The last note of craziness was contributed when, an hour out of Idlewild, they were flagged back to Gander for "a mechanical fault."

He rang her from Gander, and drew a choking breath of relief when she replied.

Chapter Two

George and Blythe Ginever never ought to have married. It took them a long time candidly to admit it, and to arrive at a more or less amicable neutrality, interrupted from time to time by the inevitable disagreements of two obstinate and opinionated people, each with a private grudge against the other—which they agreed, for the sake of peace, quiet, and good manners, to sink, but never to forget.

All her life Blythe Cherrill, as an idolised only child, had been pampered; her parents, her nanny, and a succession of governesses spared her all tiresome decisions. As the daughter of a don, Master of Ginever's own College, she might have received a good, sober education, leading possibly to an Arts degree (if she had been scholastically inclined); but her father's marriage to the daughter of a peer complicated the issue. There was plenty of money on his side (the Cherrills were rich industrialists) and on hers the power and the glory accruing to an earldom conferred on an ancestor in the reign of Queen Anne. Besides the Master's house in College, the Cherrills had a big place on Boar's Hill, where they enter-tained lavishly during the vacations.

Expensively "finished" in Paris, and brought out with the usual flourish, Blythe was expected to make, if not a brilliant, a "good" marriage. For some reason it did not take. Given all

17

the opportunities, she made nothing of them. A handsome, dark, inclined to be buxom young woman, she was perhaps too spoilt, too exigent; a few half-hearted suitors sheered off. Another reason was astutely pin-pointed by her mother.

"Blythe always liked girls better than boys; I did so hope she'd grow out of it," complained Lady Adela. "I really feel I'm to blame; I ought to have given her a few brothers to knock the nonsense out of her—but, you know, it's such a nuisance having children when you only start, as I did, in middle age! Poor thing—she never had the rough and tumble of male companionship when she was young enough to profit by it, and I always have the feeling she's not really comfortable with men. She expects too much of them. And these crazes she gets for elderly women! I'm quite sure," said Lady Adela earnestly, "there's nothing *wrong* about it, but it isn't normal for a person of her age and of course the men find it discouraging."

When the war broke, to forestall the coming danger of the women's call-up Blythe was shuffled into one of the reserved occupations. For some incalculable reason, the film companies were given priority call on the limited number of young people with secretarial training who had not got themselves into one of the services. Blythe had no sort of training, but a friend who, married to one of the chiefs of production, got her on to the office staff, where, characteristically, she proceeded to make the best use of her time; learned office routine, taught herself to type, invented a kind of slapdash shorthand, and came to be regarded in her own right as An Important Person.

Her first meeting with George Ginever took place at one of the V-E Day parties, when the fact that they were almost the only guests in civilian dress acted as a *point d'appui*.

She had just had a flaming row with her friend, the producer's wife, so she arrived in a mood of rebellion—which suited her. Unless activated by an emotion, Blythe was hand-

18

some but heavy; uniform would not have become her. She looked excellent in a dark woolen suit, starkly simple, cunningly cut, with an elaborate little hat that crushed her dark hair down over her ears which were clipped by semi-circles of what Ginever, in his innocence, took for paste; in the Ginever circle no young woman wore diamonds in that casual fashion. She was much the most distinguished person in the room; illuminated by her private anger, she created an artificial, but none the less authentic, sensation. Men and women—particularly the latter—made a fuss of her.

Practically everybody at that party had been on active service. Ginever was still at school when the war started; when he went up to Courthouse and, in due course, the call-up claimed most of his contemporaries, he got exemption on bad sight and on the results of his smash on the playing fields. His war record was inglorious, and he took the first opportunity of getting out of the uniform into which he had been pushed by the M.O.I.

He was gauche, socially insecure—and inclined to be overwhelmed by the unconcealed interest of an elegant, sophisticated young woman, moving with assurance in circles to which, if he had aspired (which as yet he did not) he would not have had the *entrée*. He was fascinated and, naturally, flattered by her attentions. His brief time at Courthouse (to which he proposed to return as soon as the M.O.I. permitted) had not brought him acquainted with the Master's daughter, and, although simple in the main, he was just worldly enough to envisage the advantages which might result from the meeting. But it was not entirely a matter of self-interest that quickened their relationship. Like many sensitive youths of uncertain background, Ginever had always been attracted towards women considerably older than himself, and was put off by the "tempo" of his feminine contemporaries. Coming to the University, and eventually to London, from a narrow, provincial circle (his father managed a little branch bank in

19

one of the mining areas), his negligible private means, as well as his personal inclination, disposed him against the pub life and party life with which the majority of his acquaintances were countering the air raids. He was trying to write. By the time he met Blythe Cherrill he had had sex with the widow of a night fighter shot down over the Channel in the winter of 1940.

According to her own account, Blythe had definitely never been "in love" before she met at that party a tall, sallow, young man, grey-eyed, bespectacled, tow-haired, hesitant of speech and shy of approach, and abruptly decided that he was what she wanted.

All her life Blythe had got what she wanted, exactly when she wanted it. The reason she had not so far acquired a husband was partly that she had never wanted any of the men who paid court to her enough to make the slight effort which the least demanding of swains is liable to expect from his mistress. She was eventually to admit, with astonishing candour, that she had never, before George Ginever's, had a proposal of marriage. It must have been her own fault; plenty of people should have been prepared to marry Blythe Cherrill, with her looks, her background, her parentage, and her money. A certain cool discouragement may have put them off. Blythe was used to having things all her own way, and there was just not *that* in her looks or her personality which inclined her admirers (they were not a few) to take the risk. Less lovely girls, less intelligent girls, less rich girls somehow found husbands. With her twenty-seventh birthday in sight, she realized that she must stop havering.

The acceptance by her family of a so far undistinguished young man who eventually had the temerity to ask her to marry him was the measure of their affection for Blythe. It was in Ginever's favour that he was old for his years—more satisfactory still, that he *looked* old for his years, while Blythe, under the influence of their mutual attachment (by then, he was very much attracted to her) suddenly began to look younger than hers. The engagement created some small sensation, and Ginever was considered to have done very well for himself. Influence swiftly procured his discharge from the M.O.I., and it was agreed he should go back to Courthouse and take his degree before he got married.

The wedding was a slap-up affair in a London church. It was given a spread in the glossies, and the shy little knot of friends of the groom was submerged in a flood of titles. Ginever felt sick and was bright yellow. Blythe, in white satin, looked matronly. To do her justice, she would have preferred not to have had a white wedding, but accepted it in deference to her mother's wishes. "Poor Adela's moment of triumph!" was whispered among friends of the bride; she had at last got her difficult daughter off, and the satin and the veil (a family heirloom) and the bridesmaids and pages were considered to celebrate her success, rather than Blythe's. They horrified Ginever; throughout the ceremony he could not rid himself of a feeling of apology towards his small, serious father and his shy little mother, and the clutch of simple relatives they had brought with them from the North: the men well clothed in their provincial dignity, which lent them assurance, the women a little overdone in the expensive gowns they had bought off the peg in Manchester or Bradford for a London wedding.

"Poor Adela's putting a wonderful face on it. It must be a frightful come-down from her ideas for that girl of hers."

" 'Poor Adela's' no fool. That young man's got a future." It was a dressing-room conversation, after the reception.

"A future, perhaps—but no past. I mean, tradition."

"You mean, our sort of tradition. A hundred years from now"—the speaker sighed—"our tradition isn't going to count for much. The young Ginevers, Joneses, Smiths—what have you—are going to build up their own tradition, based on achievement, not on inherited privilege. In my opinion, it's a good marriage—for Blythe Cherrill."

And another dressing-room conversation:

"Just imagine Blythe—Blythe Cherrill—capturing that soul-throb of a man! He's my utter pin-up!"

Blythe's parents set them up in a little house in one of the Montpeliers, the lease of which was in Blythe's name: a short lease, because it and most of the adjoining property was due for demolition. (Sixteen years later it was still undemolished.) "It won't matter," his father-in-law told him, with gratifying if slightly unnerving confidence. "By that time you'll have found something more suitable. It's getting a bit shabby round here." Shabby it might have been, according to the notions of the Master of Courthouse and his wife Lady Adela; it was a very charming little house for a young married couple, and an admirable centre for a young man preparing to storm literary London.

A year after the marriage Flavia was born. The event was followed by an extraordinary run of luck for George Ginever. In the course of four years he wrote a couple of short historical novels which, though the medium was cried down by the higher flight of critics, received favourable notices in the British and American press and sold well enough to justify the time he had spent over them. A little too literary for the common reader, they gained him respect in circles not ordinarily receptive to popular fiction, and earned him jobs in reading, editing, and reviewing. The first novel was bought by an English film company and he was invited to collaborate on the script. Sooner than in his most sanguine moments he had anticipated, he was financially independent of his father-in-law.

It gave him a considerable shock, to find that Blythe did not like that. He came gradually to realize it, by way of a few barbed remarks, and at first thought it must be, on his part, a misunderstanding. It was difficult to believe that Blythe would have preferred him to go on being dependent—not on herself, which would have involved her in responsibilities she was not fitted temperamentally to assume, but on her parents. It took him a long time to realize the truth: that, while Blythe was gratified by his successes, and contributed to them in no small degree, she disliked no longer being able to regard him as an appendage.

Yet they were happy for a year or two. Ginever was young enough to be proud of his responsibilities to a distinguished and charming wife; he was in love with her, and she from time to time—but at widening intervals—was in love with him. But she had made it clear, almost before the end of the honeymoon, that the initiative was always to be hers. In regard to the feelings of her young husband, to his masculine needs, she was ruthless: would starve him deliberately for weeks—it grew to be months—on end, and when eventually she surrendered, it was with an air of tolerance and patronage, rather as one might award a treat to a child who had behaved itself.

He tried in all the tenderest ways he could imagine to woo her, until it was borne in on him that between her infrequent emotional peaks, Blythe was not merely unresponsive, but completely frigid; that except when momentarily driven she had a positive dislike of normal husband-and-wife relationships. Deeply humiliated, he withdrew—and the outcome was to be taken for granted.

Blythe was seven years the elder—of which disparity he grew to realize she was painfully conscious, and became more so as time went on. He would have forgotten if she had not kept forcing it on him. If he so much as looked at a younger woman, it was "Gather ye roses, my dear, for all you're worth. It's a pity mine are faded." It would not have occurred to him that Blythe's roses were faded, if she had not put the idea into his head. She was even more handsome than she had been at the time of the marriage; after Flavia's birth she

23

had fined down, and with loss of weight had, so far as looks went, lost years. But the seven years of difference between her and her husband for some reason haunted her; too proud to affect youth, she assumed the style of a middle-aged woman long before she was entitled to it. She made Ginever feel a fool, not because he was married to a woman older than himself, but because she took to treating him, publicly and in private, as though he were a contemporary of their daughter Flavia.

All this could have been bridged by love, if love there had been. It took him a long time to realize there had never been love; to recognise the difference between being in love and loving.

They had been married less than four years when he was unfaithful for the first time, and it was another year before Blythe guessed what was going on. She challenged him, he admitted it, and she took it loftily. "Do as you please; but don't imagine I'll ever divorce you!" He did his best to convince her it was the last thing he desired. It was not only for Flavia's sake he did not want the marriage to break up. His Nonconformist upbringing had possibly something to do with his attitude to divorce, but there was a large element of pride in it. Divorce was an admission of failure; it seemed ridiculous that two people with so much in common as he and Blythe should not be capable of making a "go" of it. Nor did there seem to be any good reason for hurting her parents (to whom he was deeply obligated) and his own, by resorting to the courts to settle their incompatability.

After the show-down they no longer shared a bedroom, and his last hope of giving Flavia a brother or a sister petered out. They came to a courteous agreement to lead their separate lives.

Looking back, it was remarkable, the way they adjusted. Blythe helped him to prepare lectures, typed and corrected

24

manuscripts (he was then employing only a little part-time stenographer), read galleys, checked publicity—even took on the detestable task of composing publishers' blurbs. She did research for him at the Library and the Museum. She entertained for him, and, through her own pull on academic and social circles, made valuable contacts for him. And as the volume of his obligation to Blythe piled up, so the quality of their personal relationship deteriorated.

What had he done for her? It was, in comparison, so little, so much of it wholly accidental and unconscious that he was ashamed to summarise it. As his literary reputation advanced, she got some kudos out of being "Mrs. George Ginever" at first nights, premiers, and literary functions he would have cut out, but for knowing that she enjoyed them. It was probably gratifying, as "Mrs. George Ginever," to be given preference by headwaiters, to figure in gossip columns, and be invited to sit on select committees. Pretending that it was all a "great bore" or a "frightful waste of time," Ginever's suspicion that she took an almost childish delight in such ploys was confirmed by Blythe's mother—with whom by then he was on increasingly cosy terms.

"It's perfectly extraordinary, the way Mother has taken to you!"

"Well, as a matter of fact, I've taken to her."

"So it appears! But there's no need to exaggerate it!" said Blythe with her ironic little laugh. "You've taken her to a movie, lunched her at the Connaught, and taken her to the Colony—all in the last fortnight! You're turning Mamma into a giddy old lady, and cutting her completely adrift from her bridge and her girl friends."

"She only gets a few weeks off the leash in the whole year. You were dated up the day I asked her to lunch, and you hate night shows. She had never seen one, and she was thrilled to bits."

"I don't doubt it," was Blythe's dry rejoinder.

Over champagne and oysters at the Colony, Lady Adela became confidential. Ginever said something faintly apologetic about the claims he and his work made on Blythe's time and energies. Adela gave him the bright-eyed look of a bird.

"Don't let her mislead you, my dear boy. You've given Blythe what she's wanted since childhood: a sense of importance."

"But surely—she's had that all her life."

"Ha." The old bright eyes clouded mysteriously. "The wrong sort of importance. She was outrageously spoiled. That almost invariably happens to the children of elderly parents. And at the same time she lived under our shadow—very complicated," said Lady Adela vaguely. "But make no mistake: she loves every little shred of importance which comes to her through you. An odd girl, you know." One of the things he found fascinating about his mother-in-law was her curiously impersonal approach to her daughter. "She 'favours'—as they say—more her father's side than mine; excellent people. We're a bit—what's that new word?—'off-beat.' I could tell you some very amusing things."

"Please do!"

"*Un de ces jours!*" she twinkled at him, and let him light a cigarette for her, and turned her elegant small head, her elaborately framed glasses, towards the *estrade* on which now appeared the first of the cabaret turns, with the eagerness of a small child at its first pantomime.

As a girl—as a young woman—she must, he reflected, have been delicious; and tried to imagine the reason for the delayed marriage to an elderly don, that resulted in the birth of a daughter when Adela was in her middle thirties and her husband nearly fifteen years older.

When he took her back to her hotel, at the unseemly hour —for an old lady—of two in the morning, she lifted her face of a withered flower to receive his kiss.

"Thank you so much, my dear; it's been delightful." She

26

laid her small, gloved hand on his arm for a moment. "It's such a treat to come out with somebody young, who doesn't behave as if one were a sort of museum piece. Give Blythe my love.— You know what you'll have to do, if you really want to please her? Give her a title! She'd adore to be Lady Ginever. Don't tell her I said so, but she's terribly, terribly *bourgeoise*, poor darling!"

He made himself as agreeable as he could to Blythe's friends and relatives. They met on criticisms of books and plays— though their views were usually too much in accord to be stimulating. They gradually slid into a polite, uninterested relationship, and Blythe made no ado over resigning her secretarial duties to an efficient young woman who, as time went on, liberated Blythe to pursue her own interests—in what these consisted he, increasingly smothered in his own work, had no more than a vague idea. Blythe continued to run the house, to act as hostess on occasions to which she attached more importance than he. She was right; in the rat-race of the publishing world entertainment was of importance. Regarding it as a waste of time, he was not sufficiently grateful.

And so to their daughter, Flavia.

Ginever had the usual paternal mania for his infant girl; went through the inevitable stages of paternal fatuity. He was, to some extent, kept in order by Blythe, and by a competent nanny; learned not to "interfere" with the child's bath-times, meal-times, sleep-times. But a nursery routine is not easily fitted into the routine of a hard-worked writer, committed to incalculable hours. Eventually he damned the nanny, and snatched every possible moment for being with Flavia. Sometimes she slept under his doting eyes, sometimes she sicked up her food at the sheer excitement of his arrival, sometimes her bath-hour became a riot of ridiculous games

27

—"He gets her so wild," complained the nanny, "she doesn't go to sleep for hours."

When she arrived at the stage of managing a knife, fork, and spoon, and of keeping her balance, not in her baby-chair, but on layers of cushions which brought her on a level with her parents' table, there was supposed to be a ritual of Flavia's lunching on certain days in the week with her mother and father. The ritual broke down because Ginever was too often unable—for professional reasons—to fulfil this small domestic commitment. Blythe would have her own luncheon taken up to the nursery. Flavia, at first inclined to bawl with disappointment, speedily learned to be sensible. It became an event, a never-to-be-reckoned-on, but rapturous delight, to have lunch downstairs with her father; a wild thrill to be taken by Father to the Zoo, or to a Walt Disney, or to even so brief an occasion as the changing of the Guard at the Palace. These things were rare, and special, and personal to themselves, and built up an attachment between father and daughter of which Blythe was, not unreasonably, jealous.

"You have all the fun of being a parent, and I have all the hard work!" she complained.

He saw the fairness of it; Blythe had all the planning, the organising, and the disciplining, and he, to Flavia, represented the fun and games, the escape from routine, the element of the unexpected which is grateful to youth. What made him uneasy—made him see trouble ahead—was Blythe's increasing possessiveness. Having ceased to possess him, her possessive instinct was directed towards Flavia.

Their arguments started when Flavia was still in baby-school, toddling off, hand in hand with her nanny, to a kindergarten round the corner from Montpelier Square, where she met little boys and girls whose upbringing was similar to her own: who belonged to a minute, restricted, rarefied post-war stratum of the so-called privileged classes which—they both agreed—was of no good to Flavia's future in a world where privilege had ceased to exist. "But I'd like her to learn good manners and good morals while it's young enough to 'take,'" said Blythe—and he agreed with her. "Goodness knows what will come to her later on; but some of my ideas—which I suppose you'd call old-fashioned—go right back to when I was Flavia's age. Somebody said to me, when I was still in the schoolroom, that good morals are only, when you get down to it, good manners."

They discussed where Flavia was to go, after she was through with baby-school. Ginever—admitting he knew little about the subject—cited a good, slightly old-fashioned boarding school to which his sisters had gone, and come out well-educated, well-adjusted young women; there were others, the Abbey, the Chase, Mortimer . . .

"I don't want Fla to go to boarding school," said Blythe flatly. "Not, at any rate, before she's fifteen or sixteen. The Abbey and the Chase? You have to clock in while they're in their cradles! It's like getting a boy into Eton or Harrow. Besides, I believe in girls being brought up at home. No, not that nanny-governess stuff I had; I mean real school, but living at home. Mixing with all sorts, but having the stabilising influence of a normal social life, apart from that puerile nonsense of 'up the school' or 'up the house'! Getting a sense of genuine values."

It sounded very good; Ginever was in accord with most of it. He wanted no more than Blythe that his pretty girl should go to one of those expensive educational factories that turned out their sleek products, stamped "Mortimer," or "Abbey," or "Chase," infected with ideas more becoming to young men than to young women—ideas which, admittedly, quickly wore off: but what was the idea of infecting them in the first place?

As the discussion went on, it became increasingly plain that it was not a discussion but a statement; Blythe had the whole thing taped and, had he been inclined to dispute any of it, there was nothing reasonably to dispute. Flavia should spend a few years at a well-known private day-school on the fringe of the Park, "and then we can give her a year abroad before she comes out.— What are you laughing at?" demanded Blythe suspiciously.

"Nothing; go on." He was tempted to remind her that in the Ginever family the girls did not "come out"; they got good, solid educations and embarked on careers. But that would have annoyed Blythe; she would have called it "inverted snobbery."

The thought shot into his mind—how much of Blythe's scheme was planned for her own benefit and how much for Flavia's? And he was shocked that he should question the purity of Blythe's motive.

Whatever was the motive, the plan appeared to work out to the advantage of all. Smothered in work—lecturing, editing the book columns of a new, middle-brow monthly, giving talks on the BBC, churning out reviews, articles, and an occasional short story, in addition to his serious work, the novel on which he had been engaged, with the research it entailed, over the better part of three years—Flavia's passion for her new school seeped through their limited encounters. She was happy, healthy, and intelligent, ablaze with enthusiasms which she did not, like many children of her age, keep to herself, but was eager to share with her parents. The one point on which he and Blythe unreservedly agreed was that Flavia should have a happy home, undisturbed by consciousness of their private incompatability; above all, that she should never be forced into taking sides. Too many modern children grew up in a state of parental warfare, accepted the break-up of their homes with pain, which they masked with cynicism, and drifted sooner or later into the ranks of juvenile delinquency. Flavia herself was aware of it, and on at least one occasion discussed it solemnly with her father, in reference to the elder sister of one of her schoolfellows.

"Of course, Lelia's shocked everybody, and we're not supposed to talk about it, but naturally we do. She was a prefect when I was just a new kid, and I think she left the term after I came, but I remember her perfectly; she was awfully glamorous to us juniors. But, you see, Daddy, she and Betta, my friend, you've met Betta—they never had a proper chance. They've had three fathers that Betta can remember—*three!* And Lelia adored the first one—their proper father—and simply hated the other two. And when he went off—the proper one—it was absolutely the end for Lelia. Betta says the new one—the one her mother married last year—isn't so bad at all, but Lelia loathes him. Well, you can see, can't you, Daddy? If parents don't have a proper sense of responsibility to their children, the children aren't to blame if they get into messes like Lelia's," said Flavia virtuously.

"The more I see of life," said Flavia, at the age of thirteen, "the more I realize I'm lucky. You've both given me a jolly good home, and a jolly good time. I sometimes wonder . . ." Her voice faltered. He asked what she wondered.

"If anybody's got a right to be as happy as I am," she stammered, "in times like these."

This gave him a shock. Flavia was growing up in the Age of Youth; when the young were masters of the world. She was surely too young as yet to be troubled by the incalculable future. He knew suddenly that he wanted his little girl to be gay and frivolous and carefree, the way they were before the war; innocent and ignorant and trusting. What folly. Modern society, modern education had robbed modern children of all that: the social and educational climate forced them into a bogus maturity before they had had time fully to enjoy their own childhood. The forced blossom: how quickly it shrivels. What would Flavia and her contemporaries have to look back upon, of the subtle and exquisite joys of childhood? Too intelligent too soon, already perturbed by intimations of responsibilities towards which they were advancing too quickly . . .

31

At least, he consoled himself, the comedy he and Blythe had played for Flavia's benefit had apparently, in its effects, been convincing; she had "a jolly good home."

Every conceivable thing went wrong on that lecture tour he undertook in the Spring of 1961. It was his first professional visit to the United States. The tour was planned to cover ten weeks; warned by an English colleague, he had stipulated for not more than three lectures in a week. He forgot to allow for hospitality, for interviews, travel time with its attendant exhaustions, for pressure exerted by American editors whose demands, his English agent warned him, it was not politic to ignore. He enjoyed the variety and the novelty of the first six weeks, the people he met, the new scene, new ideology—but he was dog-tired and looking forward to going home when his New York agent rang him at Dallas and told him that a play of which he was part-author was going into production.

He had forgotten about that play; the London managers had turned it down, a Broadway producer had taken an option, and, having heard nothing further, he assumed the option had lapsed. It now appeared it had been renewed. But the producer wanted a lot of changes, and Ginever would have to be around. Why, he asked, could not his co-author, resident in Manhattan, do the coping? Because his co-author was on a film assignment in Venezuela. He was still reluctant, felt too tired to bother; didn't particularly care about the play, didn't, if it came to that, believe in it.

"Hell, George," came in an exasperated splutter from New York. "This is the Webbs! They aren't happy about their last play and aren't bringing it on to Broadway. They've been reading every script they could lay their hands on and for some reason Cath's taken a fancy to yours. God knows why. They've turned down a Tennessee Williams and a Rattigan. They've got the theatre and they're due to open in five weeks. There's got to be a big re-write . . ."

32

So that was that; apart from his own inclination, he owed it to Marrotti, not to let this big chance slip. Dead with fatigue, Ginever dragged himself back to New York, and spent the next month on planes—covering his lecture dates—and in fevered sessions with Leo and Cath Webb. By the time he had virtually re-written the play (with long telephone conferences with Pete Marrotti), and it had gone into rehearsal, American methods of production had brought him out in stomach ulcers. The play had (in spite of the Webbs) a tepid reception, of which Ginever was unaware; he was in hospital, being operated.

When he came out of the anaesthetic, it was confusing to see a figure resembling Blythe at the side of the bed.

His recovery was unexpectedly slow; there was not a moment of "danger," no set-backs, nothing to create anxiety. The operation was more or less of a side issue—the inevitable outcome of a pile-up of work over a number of years. All the time he was weak and sleepy, and Blythe's bored, patient presence at his bedside was an irritant he did his best, for courtesy's sake, to disguise.

It was agreed that he should take a holiday, before coming back to work. Have a long rest, and get on peacefully with his neglected novel, before coming back into the tohu-bohu of London.

"Fla's going to Lausanne after Christmas," said Blythe casually, on the end of one of their conversations.

"After Christmas? But—"

"Yes; it's sooner than we'd intended. But I'm not very pleased with the company she's keeping. They couldn't have her at the place we wanted—they seem to be booked up to the end of next year. But Oggie Schneider's got her in at that school—I forget its name—where Oggie's girl 'finished'; it sounds good."

"Oh yes.— How's Oggie?" he heard himself asking without interest.

"She's over here with me. I imagine she's having a good time; she knows dozens of people in New York."

And then the door opened, and Luce came in, with her arms full of flowers.

"Hi!—oh, I'm sorry," she said, in her dark baritone voice.

He allowed his lids to drop over his exhausted eyes.

"This is my wife. Blythe, this is Mrs. van Thal."

"I'm in the play," he heard Luce explaining. "I'm Lucian van Thal—no, I'm not in the program; I'm only an understudy. I think"—he felt her eyes covering him—"he looks pretty tired. I'll come in another time. I'm very glad to meet you, Mrs. Ginever."

"I believe you've been very kind to my husband," said Blythe formally. "You got the doctor, and got him into hospital, and all that, didn't you?"

"That's giving me too much credit! Your husband looked awfully sick, and Hartington Green—that's the doctor, as you know—happens to be a personal friend of mine, so I got hold of him, and he did all the rest.— Well, I'm sorry I interrupted; I'll give these things to somebody to put in water and see you tomorrow, if all's well."

"What an extraordinary young woman!" said Blythe, as the door closed behind Luce. "That voice! Is it always like that, or has she got something the matter with her throat?"

"It's always like that," said Ginever, wishing Blythe had gone and Luce remained, and wondering what had happened to make Luce alter her visiting time; she usually came in the evening just before the theatre.

"And do you mean to say she's an *actress?*" said Blythe, on the slight note of disparagement which usually came into her voice when she spoke of younger women. "Is she any *good?*"

"I haven't the faintest idea. I've never seen her act."

"But she said—"

"She's understudying; she said so, didn't she? We haven't

34

got down to rehearsing the understudies, and it's not my job anyhow." He knew he sounded bored and petulant. Blythe, for some reason, had become chatty. If only she would go.

"Has she got money in the show, or something?"

"I haven't the remotest idea; why should she?"

"Such an odd-looking person. She reminds me of—who was it? Oh, the Tree girl—Viola, wasn't it? I saw her in Shakespeare or something, while I was a kid at school," said Blythe vaguely. "A great, stringy lamp-post—she'd never have got parts if she hadn't been his daughter.— I suppose this Miss What's-her-name plays character?" said Blythe, putting the professional term into inverted commas.

He muttered he did not know what Miss What's-her-name played, and didn't give a goddam. He had never set eyes on her before they met at rehearsals; she was there, like the rest of the understudies, to watch the changes, and one day they had got into conversation. That was all there was to it. He closed his eyes to indicate that the subject was closed, heard Blythe rustle to her feet, and felt her gloved fingers brush his brow. He put up his hand quickly to touch hers.

"Sorry to be a bore. I'm just—sleepy."

"Have a good night. Oggie's got a party, and we're going to the play."

"Hope you won't be bored," he mumbled.

"Not very likely, with the Webbs."

The door clicked. He remembered, with a great wave of relief, that there were only two more days before she went home.

Their last conversation, on the following afternoon, was about Flavia.

"This Lausanne business; it's a bit sudden, isn't it?"

"It had to be," said Blythe, tight-lipped. "There was a bit of trouble, if you remember, before you went away."

He was ashamed that he could not distinctly remember the

35

"trouble"—something about late hours and rowdy companions, with which, as usual, he left Blythe to deal.

"We've been having words all the time, and the words became rows. We've had, actually, a wretched summer. The friends she brought down to Marlow this year were—most of them—quite disreputable. She knows it as well as I do. I got her in a good mood one day and tried to thrash it out. But she was on the defensive at once. So I told her I'd made up my mind; she'd got to go to boarding school a year sooner than we intended."

"How did she take that?"

"We didn't speak for days," shrugged Blythe.

Who to be sorry for, Blythe or Flavia?

"Do you mean to say she's said nothing about all this in her letters to you?"

He admitted, not a word. Flavia's letters were mainly post cards; such letters as came—there had not been more than three or four—were commentaries on his letters to her: "That rodeo must have been terrific. One of the things I'd really love to see.—What a ghastly place that Dust Bowl sounds.—I awfully envy you those gorgeous beaches, it's icecold and wet here nearly all the time.— You seem to have had a smashing time in Chicago.— Thanks for the records, they're absolutely smashing.— Those photographs are really super. I know you'll be bringing me a present: could it be a camera—one of those ones that develop and print in the same operation? I've read about them . . ."

There was love, but no intimate communication any longer between him and Flavia. Something must be done about that.

"This Miss van Thal—"

"Mrs.," he corrected automatically.

"Oh. I suppose she's your mistress," said Blythe.

"As a matter of fact," said Ginever, "she is not." And felt like adding, Not yet. He knew already what Luce was going to stand for in his life.

36

Chapter Three

One night when he was alone, about a fortnight before he left Oyster Bay, he read through the two hundred-odd pages he had written, so far, of his new novel. When Luce came in, he was feeding it solemnly, page by page, into the log fire.

"What are you doing?" she cried out, and caught at his arm. "Oh *no*, George!" Her thin hands clutched towards the blackened flakes. He pushed her off. He laughed.

"So what? It's caca."

"All the work—all the time you've put into it!"

"Yeah? All the work, all the time your great-aunt—was it? —put into that bloody thing"—he pointed. "That monstrous product of a third-rate mind."

Luce picked up the cushion and hurled it on the fire. A nauseating stench of burning feathers rose from the hearth. He said stupidly:

"You didn't have to do that. People have a right to their likes and dislikes. 'Now who shall arbitrate?'"

"You don't suggest I liked that object? It came to me in a box of junk when Aunt Livvy died. I'm cowardly about destroying things," admitted Luce. "I mean," she amended, "things people have made with their own hands: not turned out on some ghastly machine."

"Were you fond of her?"

37

"Of my Aunt Livvy? I was *not*. She was an old cow, and a bitch to Mamma. But—oh, I don't know how to explain it—every one of those piddling little stitches was a second in the life of a girl who was once young and vivid, and, like chimney sweepers, came to dust. Yeah; she was third, or fourth, or fifth rate, if you like, intellectually. She had all the wrong values, according to us—and we've got the wrong values, according to her." She broke off to laugh. "You've not seen my chamber of horrors upstairs. Stuff I've inherited from one side or other of the family. There was an old cousin who thought he could paint. 'Cousin Alfred—the artist!' He was always 'the artist' to Aunt Livvy and my grandmother. I look at his pictures sometimes; they're the *end*. They'll wind up on somebody's bonfire. But me—I couldn't destroy them. Every brushful is laid on with love and confidence. You can feel the good, nice, commonplace person behind them, who just wanted to leave a record of something he cared about. There was another one who wrote a novel and got it published in the eighteen-eighties—I've never managed to read the whole of it. And some amateur musicians who turned out ballads or drawing-room 'pieces.' None of them were plagued with intimations of immortality. None were artistic or literary. They were quite happy and satisfied with their bit of technical accomplishment—whatever that amounted to.

"But what's Aunt Livvy's beastly cushion got to do with —what you've been doing?" She interrupted herself. "Oh, George!" She loosened the clutch of his fingers on the few remaining pages.

"I should think the line of connection's pretty plain; they're both caca," he repeated. "Of the two, mine's the more reprehensible, because I know better. Ay, there's the rub."

"Honey." She was looking at him with genuine perturbation. "I knew you'd started working before you were ready for it. Doc Green said you oughtn't to look at a typewriter for three months at least—and you were on the job as soon as you got to Hyannis."

"I guess it's one of those compulsive things. What's the word?—push-button.— Can't keep my finger off the button." He pushed a laugh again, got up and found the Scotch and the syphon. "It's like that!" he said, as he came back with the full tumbler. "If you're an alcoholic, it doesn't mean you like alcohol. You don't even taste it. But you've got to have it. You go crazy without it. I guess that's how I've got about writing."

"You—don't—like—writing," said Luce, spacing the words. He gave her a fuddled look. He had been drinking, and had not had very much to eat, since breakfast. Luce had been out all day.

"Loathe it."

She gave a little, uncertain laugh that reminded him of Flavia when he made some remark that went slightly over her head.

"Then why—? Sorry—I know: you've said."

"Not completely. Look: go and sit over there. I want to say some things, and I'll say them better if you're not too close."

She sat obediently in a chair on the farther side of the hearth; sat relaxed and beautiful, with her head thrown back on a cushion, her thin hands clasping her left ankle, which rested on her right knee—one of her favourite attitudes. He lit his pipe, looking at her across the flame cupped in his hands. He started didactically, as if he were addressing a university group.

"There are two parts to this compulsive thing, and one is neurotic. That's actually minor and contributary; we're working backwards, from effect to cause. You establish a habit over years, and eventually it takes charge. Whether it's drink, or women, or work. Unless you've got a powerful corrective, counter-balance, or whatever you like to call it—maybe something moral, or religious, or just plain human—it's likely in the end to beat you. Imperceptibly, to start with, you're giving in to a habit. By the time you're aware of it, it's too late."

"But is it?" Her deep voice filled the silence. "Isn't that what psychiatrists are for?"

"The acceptance of psychiatric treatment," he answered, "implies a discipline for which not everybody is prepared. It's not so difficult for the simple, the primitive, the under-educated, who aren't aware of that abandonment of the—I can't find the word—the privacies of the mind, the spirit, I suppose I mean of the soul, which constitute the inner fortress of the human being. Those privacies mayn't be very creditable, but they build up something which, to you, means YOU, and to me, ME."

"And suppose," said Luce gently, "the YOU or the ME is diseased? We don't mind going to a clinic when we have a pain in our stomach, our lungs, or our liver. Ought we to mind going to a clinic when we've got a pain in our minds?"

"Not if we're prepared to accept. But, so far as I'm concerned, that implies a degree of credulity quite beyond my admittedly limited intelligence. I'd have to find a character like Jesus, like Mohammed, or Plato, or Gracián—before I'd let him tamper with my mind. I suppose I lack the total submission that the True Church requires.—"

"You aren't a Catholic, are you?" she asked quickly.

"No; I wish to God I were. I might find the answers. My bloody stubbornness stands between every sort of relief that religion and science might offer me. 'I am I'; that's a *cliché* a popular Victorian playwright put into the mouth of one of his characters and an actress of the period—I suppose you've heard of Mrs. Patrick Campbell?"

She shook her head, and the age-gap yawned momentarily between them.

"Well—yes—perhaps; dimly. I don't know much—historically—about the English theatre."

"God, you make me feel like Rip Van Winkle."

"Oh, I know all about Joe Jefferson."

"More than I do. Anyhow, Mrs. Pat—as they called her—more or less founded, and lost, her reputation on that 'I am I,' in a play by Sudermann—I never saw it; I don't even remember what it was called. Some woman's name. I wasn't born—or I was an infant. But my father used to do imitations. He'd only been to the theatre three or four times in his life—they were strict Nonconformists—but I think he could have been a pretty good actor. That play—I've got it: it was *Magda* —stuck in his mind. He used to act bits for us when we were kids. I can still hear him saying 'I am I,' in a dark, plummy voice that wasn't his at all. For some reason it made an impression on me as a child. I used to march around, saying 'I am I,' and getting my ears clocked by my sisters."

"Tell me some more," came from across the room as he fell silent.

"Oh, well"—he laughed. "The 'I' got mislaid. It happens —to a good many people."

"So far," said Luce, "effects. When do we get back to causes?"

"That's boring."

"Damn you, George Ginever; am I 'bored' with anything that concerns you?"

"I don't see why not."

"Don't be a dope," said Luce impatiently. "Get back to beginnings."

So he started with the university: with Courthouse, and the literary group he got in with, and, through them, with poets and men of letters, who encouraged him to become a writer. It did not take much encouragement; he was already aware of his own possibilities, which he took with the seriousness of his age. In his last year at Courthouse he produced a "slim volume," rather pretentiously entitled A *Critic on Criti-*

cism—of which the Master thought highly enough to contribute a brief and amusingly tolerant preface.

"I'd forgotten he was going to marry my daughter; now they'll accuse me of nepotism," grumbled Dr. Cherrill.

The touch of nepotism appeared to be justified; the essay (it was little more) sold well at Blackwell's, and achieved favourable notice in the *Times Literary Supplement* from Bladon—sometime a Courthouse man. It got four respectful lines in the *Manchester Guardian* and some fluffy write-ups in the more literary journals, one of which suggested that in George Ginever the literary scene might possibly be enriched with a future Max Beerbohm.

"My dear boy, I hope you're not letting this nonsense go to your head," his father-in-law said with concern. Ginever smiled.

"No, sir; of course I'm not."

"Bladon—a slick, tiresome chap: a time-server. Always sucking up. Only wrote that thing because he imagined it would recommend him to me!"

"I'm sorry you think so poorly of my *Critic*, sir!" said Ginever, putting as good a face on it as he could. The Master obliged with some ripe, thirteenth-century oaths, which commanded his son-in-law's respect and his (suppressed) amusement.

"How dare you, sir! How dare you! You have not, I hope, the effrontery to imagine I would have set my name to something for which I had not a—ha—at least a modified respect?"

"Certainly not," said Ginever, preserving his gravity with difficulty, and withdrew from the Presence. It was true that his little book had gained him some esteem in literary circles, not confined to the University, but a few unpleasant comments had blown his way. Affecting indifference, he repeated them to Blythe, who was instantly up in arms.

"Who said that?" she demanded, looking in her wrath like an outraged Athene. Not yet having grasped that she took any criticism of him as a direct aspersion on herself, he stared, and laughed.

"What—the *vox, et praeterea nihil?* Come, come! You don't take seriously somebody who tosses about Fourth Form tags in that irresponsible fashion."

"Who said it?" she insisted. "Wait: I'll guess. I've got it. Malcolm Mullet—that jaundiced little pseudo-James; that beastly little Redbrick product—"

"He's going to be an important writer someday," said Ginever soberly. "He's a very serious scholar and one of the best speakers we've got in the Union." She snorted.

"I've read some of his stuff and I heard him speak after Eliot's lecture—*that accent!* Why," she demanded, "do you always have to stand up for beastly people? It's weak of you. Mullet's sick with jealousy—"

"Well, that's damned uncomfortable—for him."

"Sometimes I wonder—" she burst out, and checked herself. "Darling, you're terribly easy-going. Don't you realise that some of the things you've just been repeating to me are practically libellous?"

"Oh, nonsense; there's no such thing as libel in honest criticism. Mullet's as entitled to his opinion as I am to mine."

"*Honest* criticism." She caught him up on the word. "You who've written on criticism—illuminative and destructive: do you mean to say you can't distinguish between criticism and a vicious personal attack?"

"You're exaggerating the whole thing. I'm sorry I brought it up," he muttered. "The remarks I repeated were not made in print but in a private conversation, and may have been falsified in repetition. Speech—isn't it the most dangerous form of communication? An inflection, the substitution of a *but* for an *and*, can alter the tenor of a whole paragraph: you've only got to listen to a debate in the Commons and read the report in Hansard to realise that. As a method of recording, stenography will shortly be obsolete; apart from minor slips, it can't register the vocal finesses that—at least in educated conversation—stand for the true content of what is being said. Perfect recall of words is not uncommon; perfect recall of intontions is extremely rare. There's no tape of this particular conversation; so who's to say whether the statements were made in malice or just for the hell of it? In fact, it's all a fuss about nothing. Your father was probably right when he said—or implied—that my bit of success had gone to my head." He was tired of the subject, but knew from experience that she would not drop it until she had chewed it dry.

"Yes, dear." There was something peculiarly and unfortunately irritating about Blythe's voice, when it took on that tolerant note. "But let me say something, will you? In some ways, you see, I've got a good deal more experience than you." It was her delicate way of reminding him of the age gap between them. "As one advances, one's bound to make enemies. No—please—wait"—she flung up her hand to check his interruption, but for once he ignored the gesture.

"I don't make enemies; in the first place, I'm not important enough, and in the second, I'm not that kind of person. I dislike quarrelling, even with people I don't care for. All I want's to get on with the job—"

"George." She sounded like a schoolmistress, flicking the cane at a refractory pupil. "One of the things that have to be recognised—to be accepted—in what you call 'getting on with the job' is, the more you get on, the more enmity you're likely to arouse from people who, rightly or wrongly, consider they are as gifted as you, but haven't had your 'luck.'"

"Well, that's fair enough; they could be right. Why grudge them their opinions?"

"Grudging doesn't come into it. But you can't brush them off—the way you seem to think you can do. You've got to be aware—you've got to out-smart them. This 'little friend of all the world' attitude of yours—it'll only make them laugh at you; fawn on you to your face—so long as you're successful—

44

and make mincemeat of you behind your back. *All Men Are Enemies;* I don't suppose you remember a novel called that which came out between the wars. I re-read it a few nights ago; Aldington was dam' right. If you're going to succeed you've got to make people afraid of you—"

"I hate all this," he burst out. "It's not in my character. We've come through a war—in which I suppose I'd have fought, but for my disqualification, hating every moment of it. Aldington was an embittered old soldier of the First World War, and took it out in his private relationships and his published works up to his death. My God, that man was once a lovely poet!—and spent his latter years, the years of his ripeness, in grudging and sneering and denigrating all that made up the essence of his poetry. If I had a third of his quality—"

"Don't be humble," said Blythe quietly. "You're going to be a famous writer." He flinched at the adjective. "I know it. Father knows it—he's a bit tatchy about that preface; but that isn't his fault, or yours. I made him do it—and perhaps I was wrong; he's scared of being pestered for prefaces by every Courthouse man who writes a book. But he can look after himself! When Solveig publishes your novel—"

"Solveig? Don't make me laugh."

"Tommy Solveig and I've been friends since we went as kids to the same dancing class. I asked myself to lunch with him last week and sold you to him over the best steak Diane I've had in years and a Mouton Rothschild I didn't believe existed! I'll have to teach you about wine," she ended tenderly.

"And I'll have to teach you about pubs where they give you ham and eggs and things dripping with deep, dark gravy. You're not serious about Solveig, are you?"

"Of course I am. It's in the bag. You've only got to get on with the book."

To have one's first novel accepted—sight unseen—by a publishing firm like Solveig was unnerving; was a challenge. A

45

small unease teased its way through the excitement, as the day wore on, and kept him awake long after their bedlights went out. He could hear her calm, satisfied breathing in the dark. How could a person sound triumphant, even in her sleep? All day long she had been transparently delighted with herself; she had even produced a bottle of champagne for dinner.

"Hey, what's this about?"

She lifted her glass and sparkled at him across it.

"The book, darling!—and we've got to find a wonderful title for it," she ended earnestly.

It was not so much the proverbial drop of ice that ran down Ginever's spine; it was more like a small, frozen clot of mud that settled on his stomach. He was shocked to find himself resenting Blythe's intervention on his behalf, that, on his part, was surely the ultimate ungraciousness! But supposing—just supposing—it didn't come off? A publisher of Solveig's eminence was not likely to accept a first novel by an unknown writer for the *beaux yeux* of a former playmate, unless it came up to the Solveig standard. And rejection would shatter Blythe.

Green-sick with nerves, he set to on the following morning working back over what he had already written, polishing every word and sentence, condemning whole paragraphs and at least two chapters: checking and re-checking the historical background. To his surprise, having done this, the final chapters flowed easily. His characters stood up in short, sharp strokes, mainly indicated in dialogue. He was ruthless with adjectives and economical in description. Best sign of all, when he had finished, he felt another book stirring within him.

He was too eager to get at the second book to pay much attention to the fuss the critics made of the first. "Yes, yes. But the next one's got to be better," he muttered, brushing aside the clippings Blythe joyfully laid before him. It came as a mild shock, that she was much more excited by his success than he was himself. She wrapped her arms round his neck from behind and tucked her chin down on the top of his head.

"The second won't be better; don't you know the second's always a flop? You get it over and then start all over again," she said gaily. "All the writers I know say the same thing: the second book's almost always indifferent—especially if they made a big bang with the first! The first's a sort of gorgeous accident—"

"There wasn't any 'accident' about *The Grey Goose is Dead*; I sweated my guts out over it."

"Of course you did," she soothed him. "*The Goose* is going to see you over years. Look: *Contact* wants to give you a write-up."

He condemned *Contact* with an obscene monosyllable.

"All I want's to get on with the job. I'm *not* going to flop on the next book—not if they let me alone: these pimps and panders of the book columns! What I do's private, and how I do it's private—"

"Do you know you're shouting?" her cool voice interrupted him. "Of course you don't have to do anything you don't want; but, darling, do have sense! The Ivory Tower's gone out; the legend of the 'great' reviewer who could make or break a young author in a couple of sentences died before the war. It's all rat-race, and if you're not in with the king rats and queen rats—even if you write like an angel, you've had it." She rapidly quoted a few names. "Harden's an exquisite writer, and he's lucky, now, to pick up a few TV scripts. Peveril—the most erudite critic of the theatre we've got—is banished to a provincial newspaper. Why? Why?" she demanded passionately. "Because neither of them was worldly enough to play The Game!"

"Am I worldly enough?" he asked dryly.

"No, I don't think you are; but you must let me play it for you. I will—indeed I will—if you'll trust me!"

47

"Look," he said slowly. "When—if—I get some sort of assurance, perhaps—perhaps," he repeated, "I'll dance to your flute. But I've got to prove myself. I've got to make sure I'm a real writer or what Mullet calls me—'a voice and nothing more.' Let me alone. Let me alone. Let me alone," he begged, "to find that out."

So of course she let him alone. She made herself into a bodyguard, holding off the intrusive elements that interfere with the act of creation. But always she made him aware of her impatience and her ambition. To begin with, he had neither. Like the Greeks, he was possessed by the spirit of the dromenon: the *doing*. But if you live in contact with a fever patient, you are unlikely to escape infection.

The second novel—*The Fox Is Off to His Den*—was received with reasonable respect by the critics, but it was evident within a few weeks that it was not going to prove a best seller.

"I was owing plenty when I came down from Courthouse," he told Luce, "and for all Blythe's sweet talk with Solveig I'd got a rotten contract. She was furious, but, knowing Tommy as I do now, I'm not surprised. He probably did it to teach her a lesson. I'd have come off better if I'd gone direct to Solveig, typescript in hand—which I'd no more have thought of doing than of walking into Buckingham Palace and asking to see the Queen! However—Blythe was livid, and came up with Harry Lasker."

"Another publisher?"

"A top-flight agent. I felt inclined to say, No, let me work this out myself, but it didn't seem fair to Blythe, who had put herself to a lot of trouble and not got much out of it so far.

"I'd got a wife and child, and we were living on a scale I'd never imagined." He laughed shortly. "Blythe kept urging me to go while the going was good: meet people, 'be seen around,' 'consolidate my position.' I kept on telling her I hadn't got a 'position' yet, and you can't build a sky-scraper on clinkers. Anyhow, I didn't want to build a sky-scraper; I hadn't even started to think about building. I was still, in my own estimation, an apprentice. And the more I mixed with the people Blythe pulled around us, the more I lost confidence in myself. They talked a different language, they'd got a different set of values.

"I suppose if I'd been the real thing—what my father-in-law calls 'the whole cigar'—I'd have taken myself off and left Blythe to cope, while I worked out my own problems. My bourgeois background blocked that. I was starting to feel like a parasite, living on Blythe and her parents; what I contributed to the upkeep of our home was canary seed.

"There'd been a bit of trouble about my overdraft; I didn't tell her about that. I promised the bank I'd clear it off as soon as I got my royalties on the two novels. I guessed the sales figures were pretty good; going round the bookshops my books always seemed to be on show—though I hadn't made the railway bookstalls. I'd purposely taken small advances and reckoned at least a few hundreds. I couldn't believe my eyes when I got Solveig's statement. Apart from the advances—which I'd already spent—I'd only just crawled into three figures. The sales were nothing like the notices and my correspondence had led me to expect, and there were all sorts of deductions—mainly 'extra copies.' Certainly I'd given away a lot—some to friends who couldn't afford to buy them, and some by way of 'promotion'; that was Blythe's idea, and she helped me with the 'dedications.' I had a certain amount of pleasure, later, in pointing out to her that most of this seed fell on stony ground; a few of the recipients didn't even trouble to acknowledge their copies. That taught me a lesson; I never did it again.

"We had a row that night," he went on. "The Solveigs were giving one of their parties; Blythe had been full of it for days. 'Everybody' would be there. She'd got herself something impressive from Hartnell and made me get a new dinner jacket. Solveig's weren't run-of-the-mill publishers' parties; Tommy and his wife threw them up at their place in Highgate, and, according to Blythe, there was competition for invitations. A mixture of the literary, theatrical, and musical *beau monde*, with a few titles thrown in—Tommy's very snob—and all the top-flight critics that Tommy had under his thumb: if you rated an invitation to a Solveig party, you were *in*. And at the last minute I said I wasn't going."

"I should think that hurt Blythe," said Luce gently.

"Sure." He would not describe the scene which had taken place. "But I'd got to get by myself, and think the position out.

"So," he went on, "I rang up Harry Lasker and made a date. I was prepared for some sort of a commercial cheapjack, a middleman. I took one look at the little bastard, and liked him on sight. He's a bit like Punch in the face, coloured like an over-ripe mulberry. He'd got a good Rops over his desk that gave us a talking point. We agreed Rops could have been a fine writer, school of Maupassant. Then he said, 'So what do you want?'

"I hadn't thought clearly, up to that moment. I heard myself say, 'Well—I suppose—to begin with—money.'

"Little old Harry nodded. 'A man without money is a bow without an arrow,' he said. I hadn't then come across the Gnomologia, but that sounded like rock sense. Without money I'd got no say in the upkeep of our home; in the upkeep of my daughter, Flavia. We had had quite a few arguments about Fla, and I had always given in, because Blythe was paying the piper. We'll not go into that; it just—left a bad taste in my mouth.

"Soon after I put myself on Harry's list I had so much work I didn't know where to turn. Lots of it I hated, but it paid. I discovered I'd got a horrid facility for journalism. I managed

50

to avoid the cheaper sort—as I managed to avoid the more dishonest aspects of reviewing. I hadn't a moment for writing —my sort of writing. I was solvent, for the first time since I got married; I could pull my weight—and that meant claiming some sort of authority—in our household. Someday, I promised myself, I'd write another *Grey Goose:* just as soon I'd got my finances stabilized and I could give up at least a year to research."

"Well?" said Luce, as he paused. He grimaced.

"The year never came: that's all."

"I know," she said quietly. "I've watched it with other people. 'Stop the world; I want to get off.' The world won't stop, and it's like dropping off a speeding car with a lunatic at the wheel. Unless you're a very special sort of acrobat," she smiled, "You've had it."

"I had a friend—a very special friend—who was a don at Edinburgh and a great Spanish scholar. He was a lot older than I and hadn't been at Courthouse; I met him soon after I went up, in some man's rooms—he made a great impression on me. He had the Spanish face; a face like a tragic eagle, with the cold Spanish humour behind it. He'd just started on his translation of Gracián. For some reason, he found me worth talking to. I'd got a smattering of Spanish, and he urged me to make a study of it; I'd find it rewarding. We kept contact, by letters and a few meetings. He wrote to congratulate me on my success with *Grey Goose*, and we dined somewhere. He'd finished his translation; he brought me a copy. He said nobody would read it, but it had to be done, because Gracián's got all the answers. He said it needed somebody else—somebody like myself—to put Gracián over to the Common Reader.

"I thought he was pulling my leg. I said I was a novelist, not a philosopher, and he said Yes, he knew that, I'd done a nice job with my Elizabethans. I could hardly believe my ears.

Somehow I'd never imagined Walton reading contemporary fiction. He said something about my 'historic conscience,' and I said it was a long time since I'd written a historical book; and he said Indeed, what was I doing now?"

Ginever broke off to laugh. It had seemed funny, at the time, that Walton had not seen any of his recent work; but the next moment he was glad and tried to turn the subject. Walton, however, had got an idea in his head.

"One of these days you might feel like tackling Gracián; you'll find him rewarding—though you'll have some trouble," grinned Walton, "on the erotic side. Hasn't there always to be a 'heroine'? Still, that's up to your research department. I should think it would be quite a thing, to pull off a big novel without what they call sex interest!"

"M'm; unlikely. But your own description of Gracián's low estimate of women—there could be something in that," conceded Ginever; and forgot about it until Walton's death made him re-read the *Oráculo*. There was a book in this man's life, and in the writings that reflected his life; the pronunciations of pessimism and cynicism out of which he built his armour for living, the means by which the human being could become "in every way like God." It was the kind of enormous, impossible subject at which, a few years ago, George Ginever, with all the confidence of inexperience, would have leapt.

"But you gave it up," prompted Luce, as he paused.

"I thought about it for a couple of years. I made bushels of notes and flogged through the *Discreto* and the *Arte de ingenio* in the original, and got hold of de Courbeville's translations. And then—I woke up. Supposing—even supposing—I'd got it in me to write the book of which my friend believe me capable—and of which, a few years earlier, I might have been capable—" He shook his head. "It was too late. I'd missed the connection!"

"How do you mean?"

He stared at her.

"It's plain enough, isn't it?— My father-in-law"—he switched off apparently at a tangent—"'s a witty old boy, with an astounding memory, and he knew a lot of wits in his time. He admitted the phrase wasn't his—to 'sell your potright for a birth of message'! Nicholson *ainé* was the author of that. Well: I'd sold my potright—don't you see? Whether, in the first place, I'd got a genuine potright, I wouldn't like to say; 'early works!'— Anyhow, I knew I could no more write a novel about Gracián after the stuff I'd been turning out to Harry Lasker's order than a conductor could take over the London Philharmonic after half a dozen seasons of Palm Court."

"That hurt," said Luce gravely.

"I'll say it hurt. But I realised I'd bought it.— I don't know," he went on, after a silence, "what made me tell Blythe about it. She'd been particularly sweet that evening, and absolutely delighted because we'd had a big spread in one of the glossies. The house is very small, but highly photogenic; my wife has seen to that. We had two pages in colour: hall, stairs, bedroom, a corner of the drawing room—all the razmataz. Me in study—which is actually my bedroom; me with Blythe in dining room; me, Blythe, and Flavia—family party—on stairs. All done by one of Blythe's boy friends, with a pull on this glossy—I don't remember which one of them it was. Highflight publicity!

" '*Huir la nota en todo.*' "

"What's it mean? My Spanish isn't much beyond travel talk."

" 'Flee notoriety in everything.' I found myself telling Blythe about Gracián."

"So what did she say?"

"She laughed."

That cool, rippling laugh of Blythe's, so far as Ginever was concerned, put an end to what remained of his affection for her. The gentle scepticism. The implication that he was a fool.

53

"Darling—I'm sure Gracián would make a wonderful book; but—well do you think they'd take it from *you*? It's a long time since *The Goose*, and you've built up quite a different sort of reputation, haven't you?" *You've* built it up for me, he thought bitterly. "I mean—surely isn't it a mistake, to fly in the face of an established public? I mean—your library readers won't take Gracián, and I'm afraid, darling, the critics won't take you seriously. Perhaps you could have done it, in your *Goose* period; but that's a long time ago. You've made a name," said Blythe earnestly. "You're an important writer." What, he wondered, did she mean by "important"? " 'Know thine own limitations'; doesn't that make sense?"

It did make sense. So much sense, that, having abandoned the idea, he made up his mind, come hell or high water, to write the Gracián book. And possibly his publishers would not accept it. But just to write it had become, for George Ginever, something involving his honour.

He conveyed this to Luce in clumsy sentences. She nodded slowly.

"I'm not very educated. I—like—truth," she said, spacing the words out, "in rather simple language. I dislike most of the modern novelists; I can't use their vocabulary. I hate their convoluted way of thinking, and their amorality and cynicism. Oh God—their dreary 'cleverness'! I like Jane Austen, and the Brontës, and George Eliot: there's something limpid about them—"

"Hi! You can't expect me to match up with Jane and Charlotte and Mary Anne!"

"Oh well, you do, in a way," said Luce vaguely. "You've all got a clear set of values—of course you aren't as good as *them*; but you've got their sort of simplicity. Oh, behind all that tripe you write and talk, you've got it. Don't tell *me*," said Luce. "The belly-achers, like your Jeffrey Eddows and your Amberley Fry—they come over here on lecture tours, and the women's clubs eat 'em up. We're horribly naïve; we go for 'culture,' from Europe.

"How should I know if you can do your Gracián book? From all you've told me, you can't write anything valuable until you've straightened out your life. Poets and painters and musicians, down the ages, have created '*quand-même*.' You—no."

"You mean, I haven't got it?"

"You haven't got that special brand of egoism. Honey, I don't know the first thing about writing. Until I met you, I'd never even heard of Gracián. But I'm perfectly certain the first thing you need, to write a book like that, is serenity."

"You've given me that."

"No, I haven't. I've given you"—she hesitated—"a happy interlude."

"That's all it means—to you?"

"Maybe"—her kind, wide smile glittered at him—"we could call it a happy prelude!"

"That's more like it." He gave a sigh of relief.

They talked for a while very quietly, and all she said was in tune with his heart. Whatever in future he might write, he must be at peace with himself. He might never achieve Gracián; but, to keep faith with himself as a writer, he must be at peace. That meant being at peace with Blythe and Flavia. Above all, with Flavia.

Chapter Four

Christmas Day that year fell on a Monday. The deadness of British Sunday lay on the Square; rugged-up cars made a funeral procession round the curbs, a drab little family party that included a small boy snivelling on account of his chilblained knees scuttered through the cheerless dusk to the bus stop round the corner. Not a holly berry or a bit of tinsel in sight; the British believe in keeping their Christmas cheer strictly private, behind their drawn curtains. As the taxi groaned away, leaving Ginever fumbling for his latchkey, it was like being marooned on a frozen block of lava.

There was a light over the transom, otherwise the house appeared to be in darkness. He had rung through from the airport, but got no reply. Not a very enlivening homecoming; still, it was Christmas Eve, and they could have gone to a concert or a cinema. The delays on the flight had no doubt cut into their plans, and Blythe, a great one for planning, had sensibly decided to carry on.

It would have been fun to drive Flavia down Park Avenue, to show her the endless vista of Christmas trees and the monster one on Rockefeller Center; and the window displays along Fifth and the Santa Clauses jangling their handbells and all the garlanded cliff-dwellings with little lit-up trees in every window. To a child of Flavia's age the colossal racket of New

57

York Christmas, seen for the first time, would be a combined super-pantomime, super-musical.

There was a pile of Christmas mail on the hall table and a flower arrangement in a china pot, still in its shroud of cellophane, as it had come from the shop. After Flavia graduated from baby-school, Blythe said Christmas decorations made too much work for everybody; it was all very well if you had a staff to cope, but sliding on berries and getting prickles down the back of your neck did not add appreciably to the amenities of the season. So a few neat set pieces and a small neat tree were ordered from the stores, the tree to top the pile of gifts that were all packaged and beribboned before they left the shop, so that there was nothing to do but sign the attached cards—"Love to Daddy from Flavia," "Mummy to Flavia," "Lots of love from Guess Who!", "Happy Christmas, darling," "G from B," "Dear Mrs. Roberts from Fla." It always struck Ginever as rather a dehydrated and packaged Christmas, but to Flavia, having grown up in the age of dehydration, it was no doubt natural. He always did up his own parcels and they looked clumsy and messy among the rest. "Oh, George; why don't you let Ann do that up for you!" said Blythe, pretending to laugh, but annoyed underneath, because she hated having her picture spoiled. But it suited him to be stubborn about this one small thing.

He thought of the snow lying thick by now on Oyster Bay, of Luce in her parka and ski-boots, tramping out to the woodpile for logs and her big room full of dogs and young people living it up with snapdragon, holly, and mistletoe, childish games and, as the night wore on, carols. "With luck, there ought to be some skating over the weekend," they were saying when he left. It was the sort of Christmas he would have liked for Flavia. At some time or other he had promised her a Christmas at the sports, but it had never come off; his work got in the way, Blythe hated Switzerland and hated every form of sport except that which could be indulged in warm climates

58

or in a gymnasium. And Flavia, she said, was not yet old enough by herself to join a party.

He pushed open the door of the dining room, switched on the lights, and saw the table already elaborately laid: eight places. Startled, he wondered who was expected for dinner. But the time was already after seven, and there was not a sign or sound of anyone in the house. Darkness came up the stairwell from the basement when he leaned over—and it dawned on him that these preparations were not for that night, but for Christmas Day.

"Well, I am damned!" said Ginever aloud. So this was how he was received after a six months' absence and an abominable journey. Blythe and Flavia apparently out for dinner and he evidently expected to look after himself. He was so angry that he felt inclined to walk straight out of the house and go and spend the night at his club. He happened to catch sight of himself in a looking glass—travel-tired and unkempt, he could not in that state present himself at the Savile. He went furiously back into the dining room, found the Scotch, poured himself half a tumblerful, gulped it neat, and shuddered. He and most of his companions had been drinking steadily ever since leaving Idlewild and his mouth was foul.

He put the glass down and mounted to the first floor, putting on more lights as he went. The drawing-room door stood open and there were more party preparations: furniture placed with consideration, flowers spouting from vases, the tree, the parcels.

Across the landing was Blythe's bedroom, and the bathroom they shared—he on sufferance; house-trained, he had learned not to splash soap, to leave no wet towels or bath mats around, to keep his own paraphernalia in a separate cupboard. Sometimes for convenience he used Flavia's bathroom, up on the attic floor.

Over the drawing room was his bedroom, which was also his study, with a dressing room adjoining. He had discussed

59

the installation of a shower, but for some mysterious reason connected with the obsolete Victorian plumbing and the fragile condition of the building, the idea had to be abandoned; the monstrous estimate he was given for overhaul and replacement of pipes and drainage was absurd, as the house was marked for demolition. The enforced intimacy of sharing a bathroom was distasteful to them both, but particularly, he knew, to Blythe; it was only just rendered tolerable by his frequent absences from home.

The opposite room on the same floor as Ginever's was originally Flavia's, until she demanded more space, and Blythe converted the two attics into a big bed-sitting room, where she could entertain her friends and live her own private life without inconvenient intrusions on those of her parents. Her former bedroom became the library and office; so that the middle floor belonged exclusively to Ginever and his secretary.

He would have a bath, and shave, and then see what he felt like; he was not at present inclined to trail up to the West End, but he remembered a little grill in Knightsbridge which served a good steak and excellent coffee; it was not more than five minutes' walk.

A bar of the electric stove in his bedroom was actually on; he saluted it ironically—knowing he was a little drunk. And his old mohair robe was draped over the radiator in the dressing room; he pulled its warmth about him. "Well, well. Fancy you—after all these years!" he murmured inanely, and was making for a bath when he heard the distant trill of a bell.

At first he thought he would let it ring; then a sudden impulse to relieve the solitude of the house with no matter what company made him look in the glass, swipe a brush across his hair and run downstairs, inventing excuses for the dressing gown.

The visitor wore a dirty duffel coat and was bandaged up to the nose in a thick beige scarf, across which a pair of startled eyes, big and grey, with womanish lashes, stared at

60

Ginever with an expression of alarm. Whatever those eyes had expected to see, it was surely not a tall, thin, dressing-gowned figure, vested in the authority of the householder. At first glance, Ginever was not sure if the stranger were male or female; unwashed dark hair sprouted over a forehead peppered with pimples and the skin-tight jeans could of course belong to either sex. As his glance travelled down to the feet, he settled, however, for male. The youth mumbled something into his scarf and the result came out in steam round his ears; the only audible word was Flavia.

"She's out. I'm her father; can I take a message?"

Winklepickers stubbed at the doorstep; distrust flowed out of the visitor. He appeared to be speechless. Ginever shivered, he had nothing much on under his robe. He said, to be amiable:

"Come in, won't you?"—and wondered where to find some beer. It seemed obligatory on Christmas Eve to be hospitable to a friend of Flavia's.

Ignoring the invitation, the youth shoved a flat package at him, growled "You can say it's from Bull," floundered down the steps, and was swallowed in the blur of lamplight and fog.

He slammed the door and added the parcel to the pile on the hall table. So now for the bath.

He hesitated at Blythe's door. He did not wish to be caught in occupation of her quarters if she arrived back unexpectedly and wanted to dress. So he went on up to Flavia's floor, pushed the door open, and entered on chaos. All the lights were on; the slope of the roof had concealed them from the pavement. The bed was unmade and pulled out at an angle to face the TV she had been given for her last birthday. Switched on and forgotten, bands flickered across the screen and crackling noises issued from its bowels. He turned it off and picked his way through a welter of garments, record albums, film magazines, and Christmas cards to the bathroom. The tub was full of some sort of greenish dye with bits of

61

silk or nylon floating in it; he identified panties and a brassiere—the latter gave him a slight shock. During his absence Flavia had graduated to brassieres. You don't casually avail yourself of the privacy of an adolescent daughter as you might of a child's. Impossible to disturb Flavia's dyeworks—so he would take a quick tub downstairs and hope to be out before Blythe came in.

While the taps were running, he became aware of an unfamiliar fragrance in the air.

Blythe always professed to dislike heavy scents, the gardenias, Roman hyacinths, and fancy-named exotics to which the average woman of fashion is addicted. She had a scent of her own, which she had used ever since she came out, as a girl of seventeen, a frail thing specially made up for her by a famous *parfumeur*, which flavoured her bath essences and the stuff she sprayed on her hair. It was cool and fresh, charming for a pre-war débutante, but rather colourless; it had no more character than a good lavender water, and Ginever, whose taste was for rich, spicy scents—on the right people—had tried a few times in their early days to persuade her to experiment with something more interesting—going so far on one occasion as to bring her back a sample from Paris which he had asked a Frenchwoman, elegant and sophisticated, to help him choose for her.

"First you must tell me about your wife. How tall is she? What colour are her eyes—her hair? Is she *bien coiffée*? Of course she is; it is impossible to imagine you married to a woman who is not—what is that funny English phrase? 'Well turned out.'" She grimaced. "Excuse me that I make a face; it is such an ugly description—it is like machinery. *Alors*," she resumed, "what are her interests? *Le sport, la couture, les arts?*"

He sketched out what he thought was a very fair impression of Blythe: her appearance, her character, her mentality—and was disconcerted to find his companion weeping with laughter. He was a little offended; it had not been his intention, to make a laughingstock of Blythe.

"Oh, you must forgive me—but it is so funny," she gasped. "You lying there, with nothing on at all—describing your wife as if you write a chapter in one of your *romans!*— But it is good, very good indeed," she made herself serious. "I now know exactly how she is, your wife: tall, admirable figure—*peut-être un peu d'embonpoint?*—but that gives dignity . . . The scent will be sent to the hotel in the morning; and now, *mon ami*," she concluded, "please get up and get dressed, for I have a date at your Embassy!"

Blythe, presented with the crystal flask, sniffed it doubtfully, rubbed a drop on her hand and burst out laughing.

"So that's my personality, is it!"

"I think it's good and—yes, quite like you."

"Well!" She pushed the bottle back at him. " 'As others see us!' I'm afraid you'll never get me to change *my* scent," she said with the pride that always irritated him; why did she consider it a virtue, never to change her opinions? "But I'm sure one of your girl friends will adore it!"

Well; it was plain that somebody had altered Blythe's ideas! Steeping in the smooth water, he wondered, without particular curiosity, who it might be. All that concerned him was that if, after all these years, she had found a lover, it would simplify matters all round. He sat up, with a swish of soap round his shoulders, and let out a quiet whistle. By God! This was the last thing on earth he had anticipated . . . then he realized the folly of allowing his desires to run so far ahead of his common-sense: on the strength of an alien scent in his wife's bathroom to assume some clandestine attachment. Nevertheless curiosity drove him through into the bedroom. An absurd figure, draped like a senator in the bath towel, he bent over the dressing table, with its load of bottles and jars and powder bowls: taking out a stopper or unscrewing a lid to sniff. No. There was no trace here of the new influence—and, to judge from a collection of pink cartons on a chest, Blythe had been stocking up on her usual cosmetics.

He jerked himself upright; a pretty figure he would cut, if she were to walk in here, and find him fingering her belongings. Ashamed of himself, he was making for the door, when the telephone rang. Blythe's was one of four extensions. He went back, dropped on the side of the bed, and, in the act of lifting the receiver, was aware of a puff of the intoxicating scent coming up at him from the lacy pillows.

He gave the number and heard coins drop; the caller was evidently speaking from a public call box.

"Hello, Fla."

Before he could speak another voice cut in.

"Hello."

"Have you got Bull round there?"

"I have *not*."

"Well, where is he?"

"How should I know?"

A pause, then—

"We're going round to Polly's. Are you coming?"

"No. I've got a date."

"Who's your date?"

"Oh—Christmas and all that. My father's coming back from America."

"What a stinking bore. Aren't you coming to—"

He hung up; he did not want to hear Flavia's answer. He waited for the "ping" to tell him the speaker had cut out, went out on the landing, and whistled. Whistled again.

"Daddy!" came in a shriek from overhead.

She came down like a swallow and flung herself into his arms; burst into a flood of incoherencies.

"How awful—when did you get in—nobody here—how simply ghastly—I only went out for a minute—I heard the bath running—I thought it was Mummy—we kept on ringing the airport and they kept on saying the flight was delayed—"

64

"You've grown," was the only—and idiotic—thing he could find to say. It was a shock, to have left a chubby little girl, loaded with puppy-fat, and come back to a long-limbed sylph with hair in a pony-tail, a sweater halfway down her thighs and skin-tight jeans. She looked as if she could do with a wash; he lifted one of her hands to kiss it jokingly, and the nails were a dark, shiny crimson, at odds with the little un-made-up face and unkempt hair.

"What's the time? I haven't a clue; I'm awful about time. I meant to be all dressed up—oh dear, it's awful. Have you had a drink? I mean—" She giggled—

He assured her seriously that he had got himself a drink and had a bath and was about to get dressed. She hugged him.

"Oh, *Daddy!*"

"By the way, you've had a caller." His arms still round her, he felt her stiffen.

"Who?"

"Name of Bull."

"Oh, him. What did *he* want?"

"Left you a parcel. It's downstairs."

"Thanks," she muttered, dragged herself out of his arms, and fled, not down but up.

When he was dressed he called up to her.

"Hi; come down and have a drink."

"Coming; don't wait," floated from above.

He went down to the dining room and poured himself an-other Scotch, diluting it this time, and a sherry for Flavia, who presently joined him. Ginever drew in a breath. The beatnik kid who had rushed upstairs came down in a full-skirted frock the colour of rubies, with make-up splashed some-what liberally about her sweet face. He dutifully admired the effect and she flashed small white teeth at him.

"Tell Mummy that; she says this dress is too old." In-wardly agreeing with Blythe, he made a further complimentary remark which drew a giggle from Flavia. "It's silly, to dress up for supper in the kitchen: but—you coming home—it's a sort of celebration, isn't it? We're having supper downstairs, d'you see, because it's easier; Mrs. Roberts and Rita and Ingrid are off tomorrow, of course. But there's a smashing casserole and —guess what: champagne!" She beamed. "We didn't think you'd mind a party in the kitchen, on your first night home."

Chattering like a budjerigar, he became aware that Flavia was for some reason on the defensive. The hands of the clock stood at five minutes to nine when she said: "I suppose I'd better give Mummy a ring. I suppose she's forgotten the time."

"Do you know where she is?"

"Oh, I suppose at Mrs. Schneider's," shrugged Flavia. "She usually is at this time in the evening."

"How's Oggie?" yawned George; it was only something to say; he didn't care, he was hungry and he wanted to get to bed. Standing between him and the door, Flavia brushed off the enquiry.

"Did Bull Dawlish leave any message?"

"Bull—? Oh, that boy friend of yours. No, he was rather inarticulate; he only said—"

And then the latch clicked in the hall, and Blythe swept in—flowing, radiant: a loved woman, if ever there was one!— and lifted her cheek for his kiss. The kiss, on Ginever's side, was respectful; since their last meeting, in the hospital in New York, something had happened to Blythe. She flung off her coat.

"Not a taxi to be had in all London. What can you expect —Christmas Eve. I'm so sorry. You must be dead, aren't you? Fla darling, go and put the soup on. Yes, of course, a drink: gin and something—a martini. Well!" She lifted the glass he put into her hand. "Here we are again!"—a clownish parody which embarrassed him, as it did not become her. "I must say you look awfully fit, considering. It's really very nice, to have you back, George." It was perfectly sincere, and the kind

66

of thing one said to an old and valued friend; hardly to a husband. But it seemed to indicate a friendliness that boded well for the future. He felt more affectionate towards Blythe than he had felt for years.

"Let's go downstairs and you can talk while I get the meal on. I hope you're not still on your bland diet?"

The kitchen was very pretty and glittering: flowers on the table, champagne—as promised by Flavia—in the ice bucket.

"Well, how's everybody in New York?"

He indicated that they were as well as could be expected: bearing up wonderfully, considering all things, under the strain of his departure.

"And your actress friend—Lucy something? I've always meant to write and thank her, but I never seemed to get down to it. But I did send her a Christmas card."

"She'd appreciate that." Luce had not told him—or, more likely, had not yet received it.

During this conversation Flavia stood with her back to them, silently stirring something on the stove.

"Well, go on; tell me some more." Blythe pulled off the little fur hat she was wearing and shook out her hair.

"Very nice," observed Ginever.

"This old hat? I've had it years!"

"I meant the hair." She had had it lightened, or brightened, and cut into the bouffant style all the women were wearing that year. "It suits you."

Flavia gave him a look across her shoulder. Blythe flung her hair back with a gesture which was probably not intended deliberately to indicate her indifference to his opinion.

"Hair gets so tatty in the winter. I thought it was time I did something!"

"I like that sort of coppery grey. It's odd. It's different. It goes with the new scent," said Ginever, to let her know he had noticed.

"What new scent?" Her surprise sounded genuine. She had

67

opened her handbag; she held it up for him to smell. "You know I never play about with new scents."

"Oh—" said Ginever, a little disconcerted. "I thought you'd been trying something different—in the bathroom."

"Look out for that soup!" She leapt at the stove and snatched a pan out of Flavia's hand, so roughly that its contents splashed a little; a few drops went on the ruby-coloured skirt. Flavia cried in a shrill, furious voice:

"Look what you've done!" and burst into tears.

"I'm sorry, but it's your own fault; if you'd got to wear that dress tonight you could have put an apron over it."

"If you hadn't pulled the pan away—"

"If I hadn't pulled the pan away the soup would have been all over the stove—. Now will you please," said Blythe in a reasonable voice, "stop acting like a baby and go and put something else on.— I'm sorry about that," she said, as Flavia whirled across the kitchen, and they heard her high heels clattering on the stairs. "But it was really very silly of her to dress up, knowing she'd got to help with supper. Come on, we won't wait; I'm sure you're ravenous, and so am I. Deal with that, will you?" she said, pointing to the champagne.

"Well—finished the book?" she enquired on rather a forced note of gaiety, while he fiddled with the wire. He mumbled No, he hadn't, and was aware, without looking at her, of the upward twitch of her eyebrows.

"No?"

"No, I haven't," he repeated, trying to keep irritation out of his voice. "Why?"

"Darling," she reproached him. "I was only wondering! I'm not surprised—really. It's not my business, of course; but I wouldn't have said Hyannis and Oyster Bay were the best places for concentration—what with this and that," she concluded, with the elephantine tact that set Ginever's teeth on edge. "However: now you're home you can settle down and get on with the job. I saw Peter the other day"—"Peter" being

68

the publisher to whom he had graduated from Solveig—"he sent you his love and said they're waiting for the title for their Spring List. He and Mary are coming to dinner next week, but I promised you'd ring him as soon as you got home."

"Look—" began Ginever. "Never mind; nothing," he muttered. This was not the moment. He gulped his soup. Blythe looked at him curiously; he could feel her look, and the old, familiar sense of compulsion. Felt resistance bank up in him.

She cleared the soup bowls and Blythe put the casserole on the table. Ginever got up abruptly.

"I think I'll just go up and see what's going on."

"I wish you wouldn't!" burst out Blythe. "It's too bad of her to play up like this, tonight. Well, you've had a sample of the kind of thing we're putting up with these days, and I suppose she thinks she'll get away with it because you're here. Please leave her alone, let her get over her sulks, and she can come down and have her supper after we've finished."

"I'd like her to have supper with us." For once he was obstinate. As he went towards the door she called after him:

"I do hope you are going to back me up with Flavia. I've been having a very difficult time and I'm very nearly fed up. The sooner we're separated the better!"

"When does she go away?"

"Not for nearly a month," said Blythe grimly.

Flavia, in a petticoat, was sponging the front of her dress; she turned a calm, cold face over her shoulder towards him.

"No, thank you, Daddy. I don't want any supper," she repeated. "I'd be sick at the sight of supper!" she exploded, when he went on trying to persuade her.

"Well, all right; but come down and have some champagne."

"I don't want champagne, thank you"—in a painfully adult voice, that reminded him of Blythe.

"Well—thanks for my welcome home." He saw her bare shoulders flinch, and tried to press his advantage. "Look,

69

honey; in less than twenty minutes it's going to be Christmas morning."

Her head dropped, and he thought he had won. He went to put his arm round her, but she moved quickly aside; he saw her fingers clench on the ruby-coloured stuff and her whole body stiffen as she turned to look him in the face.

"I hope you'll have a happy Christmas. And you can tell my mother goodnight."

She hates Blythe, he thought.

Underneath the shock of the discovery ran a great pity for Blythe. In all the years of his unfaithfulness, he had been able to depend on the attachment between Blythe and Flavia to fill in the gap his own defection had left in Blythe's life. Blythe had never said or done a thing to turn Flavia against him; so Flavia's devotion to him had never been disturbed. But something, during his absence, had happened between her and Blythe. It was hard to imagine that Blythe had been fool enough to do something, enter on some relationship, which Flavia would interpret as disloyalty to her father. It could be no more than this complicated, feminine business of "growing up" that had made the rift . . .

He was too tired to think. He went downstairs and told Blythe that Flavia had gone to bed.

"I thought as much. Oh God, these moods!— Eat up, and let's turn in. You look half dead!—no wonder."

They yawned through the remainder of the meal, and, soon after midnight, exchanged "Happy Christmasses."

Chapter Five

In his dream Luce was standing in her favourite position, with her ankles crossed and her elbow on the mantelshelf. She lit a cigarette and tossed the match on the fire. The wiry mass of her hair concealed from him all but a small, grey segment of her face.

"I've been thinking. About that Paris notion. I don't think it's so good after all."

"So you're backing out?"

"Don't say it like that. I mean—it's just not possible to make plans before we know what Blythe's reaction's going to be. If she refuses to divorce you . . ."

"Is it going to make any difference?"

"To how we feel—no. To how we act . . . look: I've told you. I'm the child of a broken marriage. I was a bit younger than Flavia when my mother refused to divorce my father, because it went against her puritan upbringing. He couldn't honestly bring a thing against her—desertion, or mental cruelty, or any of the jazz that counts in the States for grounds of divorce. Anyhow, he'd got a crook advocate, and they pulled it between them. My brothers and I adored Father, but we were obliged to side with Mother; she'd had a raw deal, and her British blood just couldn't take it.

"I was the youngest. When my brothers got married, I

couldn't face up to living alone with an unhappy and embittered woman who wanted to possess me, because I was all she'd got. She'd had some good chances of re-marrying, and refused them because she considered herself still married to my father; she went on maintaining the divorce was illegal. I can't tell you what it was like at home . . .

"So I ran away. I went on the stage, and hated it so much that I married the first man who proposed to me. Not an actor: I'd never have married an actor. I just wanted to get away from home, and then away from the theatre.— He was a good guy," said Luce quietly. "You couldn't call it marriage; we were both too young to know what marriage meant. The way it turned out was best for both of us. Death's final, at any rate.

"Let's not make plans," she said.

He came out of sleep to Blythe, standing by the bed with a tray in her hands. Tall and thin in her wadded housecoat, her hair bandaged with a dark rose net over the ironmongery of rollers, her make-up still in its elementary stage of powder and lipstick, she looked older than on the previous night. She put down the tray and went in a business-like way to switch on the electric fire and pull back the curtains; the windows, filmed with condensation (he had forgotten to open them before he went to bed), gave no clue to the day outside. She came back, kissed her finger, dabbed it on his unshaven cheek, and told him not to let the coffee get cold. Catching sleepily at the skirt of her robe, he asked what she thought she was doing; where was the "help"?

"At home, presumably cooking its turkey. Christmas, and Easter, and Whitsuntide, and what have you," said Blythe dryly, "are now proletarian festivals. Strictly. 'Our' Mrs. Roberts, 'our' Rita, and 'our' Ingrid don't live in, and they've got their own families to look after. Not to worry. I've got a cook and a parlourmaid laid on for lunch and two men coming to look after the party tonight. There's a lot to be said for living in South West 7!"

"Sit down a minute. Have a cigarette." He pushed the box at her. She hesitated, then dropped into the armchair, lit the cigarette, and smiled with gentle irony at the smoke streaming on the air. From the table at his elbow he collected a small parcel. "There's your Christmas present."

"Oh—I've put yours under the tree.— My word! You were smart, getting that through the Customs. Thank you very much, George, it's lovely." In the mixture of chill daylight and electricity, the diamonds made a small blaze on the lapel of her gown. Luce's choice, it had cost him a handsome sum at Arpel's. It amused him to think she would have received a trinket from Woolworth's no less graciously.

"I'll be up in ten minutes. Tell me what I can do."

"Stop in bed and finish your sleep out. I'll send Fla up with yesterday's papers: I don't suppose you've seen them. Clark's column is quite good—with some compliments for you. Lunch is at two, and Pa and Ma will be here soon after one, unless they're held up by fog. If you're down in time to do a travel talk while we're dishing up—that will be more help then anything."

Propped against the pillows, he stared round the room, inhumanly tidy after his long absence. Apart from the divan bed, its main furnishing was the enormous flat desk and Regency armchair which took up the whole of the window embrasure. The walls were blocked in ceiling-high with bookshelves, just leaving space for his favourite Matthew Smith over the fireplace. A stack of pictures stood in a corner, and the easel on which he usually kept two or three was empty.

Flavia shot in with "Papers, Daddy. Merry Christmas." She gave him a smothering kiss. "Sorry about last night," she mumbled—and was gone before he could utter his own greetings.

73

Before he went to America they had had the last of many arguments about the stupidity of continuing in the little house which fitted them like a glove, but provided no accommodation for living-in staff. His literary agent, Harry Lasker, came up with a gem of a house in Islington, pure Regency, with a coach house that would have converted into a flat for a married couple and accommodated the cars for which he was now paying exorbitant rent seven or eight blocks away.

No. The house was Blythe's and she wanted to keep it, although this meant dependence on dailies, whose private and personal lives invariably took precedence of the convenience of their employers. She pointed out that he had got his study and the office, that they could seat ten (at a pinch) in the dining room and that the drawing room was spacious enough for "reasonable" entertainment. "If you want to give big parties we can do them at the Dorchester or the Savoy." She implied that he was suffering from a rush of success to the head, and did not seem to understand that all he wanted was reasonable comfort for the three of them: the kind of comfort a small terrace house could not supply. In this, oddly enough, he had the support of his parents-in-law. The Master and Lady Adela both agreed that he should, for the sake of his work, take over a more spacious establishment than that with which they had endowed their daughter on her marriage.

For several summers he rented a furnished house near Marlow—mainly for Flavia and her friends. Then he had the offer of a small but handsome manor on the Berkshire downs, at a knock-down price. It would have been ideal for his work; they could have entertained—in moderation—at weekends, and communications with town would have been easy. No. Blythe did not want the responsibilities of a country house, the business of engaging servants who stayed a few weeks, then folded their tents like the Arabs. Basically, he suspected, she did not want a house that did not belong to her, over which, therefore, she had not complete authority.

He ought to have put his foot down. But how does one put a foot down when one is conscious of overwhelming obligation? He owed Blythe too much altogether; most of the contacts which had advanced him, directly or indirectly, in literary circles, had come through her. Blythe knew, or was known by, everybody; she could ring up an editor, a publisher and get attention, because most of them had been, at some time or other, her guests. She was notable as a hostess. He owed her . . . what didn't he owe her?

He found he was working himself into a state of puerile irritation, and opened one of the newspapers, only to throw it down again. There was no good reason for stopping in bed; if they wanted him out of the way, he could find plenty to occupy him in the office. There was the mail to open—bushels of it, arranged in classified piles by his secretary, Ann Maxton, who had left a note on top ot it: "Welcome home and Happy Christmas. Stopping with friends at Epsom—address and telephone number as above. Blythe said I could take Boxing Day off but shan't be doing anything special so ring me if you want anything." There was a parcel in Christmas wrapping, which he pinched and guessed to be the usual gloves from Swayne and Adeney. Luckily he had brought her something pretty—chosen by Luce.

Luce . . . He looked at his watch. He had tried to book the call for eleven, but the lines were loaded up to two.

Now to shave and dress—and then perhaps he would take a stroll across the Park to Harry's, just to say Hello. Harry had an enviable apartment in one of the little old squares off the Bayswater Road. There would be a great welcome at Harry's, but he must take care not to get caught up in a session, and forget the in-laws at one o'clock. It would be an idea to give Harry a ring.

He lifted the receiver and found Blythe on the extension. It was at least a couple of years since Ann said, "Wouldn't it be a good idea if we had a separate number?" with which he agreed in a half-hearted way; then, when Ann said she would get straight on to the GPO, wavered about it. He knew his procrastinations strained Ann's patience, but he was made that way. So nothing was done, and Blythe's calls continued to cut into his, or vice versa. So he said he would have a separate line, and for some reason Blythe took umbrage.

"What for? I don't spend my time chattering on the telephone" (true enough) "and I do my ordering early in the morning. It can't do Ann any harm to take a message for me, and I can take your messages if you both happen to be out."

His only support came from Flavia.

"Oh do, Daddy, for goodness' sake, have a separate number! I have to tell all my friends they mustn't ring me up, for fear of disturbing you, and I'm always rushing out to the box, and it's such a bore!"

But Blythe took it as an affront—and the house belonged to Blythe.

Why was he so pusillanimous? Because he did not care. He never answered the telephone himself when he was working. It seemed to be a fuss about nothing.

He found he still had the receiver to his ear. Blythe's voice came through, like silk, like honey.

"Yes, darling one.— No, don't ring me; I've told you the set-up. I'll ring you, I promise—"

He hung up, quickly and silently.

Little old Harry, shrewdest and sharpest of the agency gang, at whose name publishers were said to cross themselves and call on their protective deities, flung open the door and his arms round George Ginever.

It crossed Ginever's mind that he owed even Harry Lasker to Blythe. In some dimly enlightened moment, the Master had accepted someone's advice to entrust his Medicean manuscript to Harry: with the result that a book which, appearing under the imprint of one of the smaller publishing houses, might have achieved a sale of a couple of thousand, ran into five figures—counting English and foreign sales—before establishing itself as a standard Penguin.

"You want the best authors, we have them," was the Lasker slogan. Nakedly on the authors' side, the most penurious of publishers found it paid to play in with him. He drove knife-edged bargains, and never touched an author in whom he did not believe. He fed the magazine market with what he thought it deserved: authors have to live! But his great pleasure was to handle "difficult" stuff. His interest in the private lives of his clients ran parallel with his interest in the business. It was George Ginever's luck to be one of his favourite authors.

They drank champagne cocktails and wished each other a happy Christmas. After personalities, Harry got down to business.

"Before you start getting yourself involved, we've got to have a session," he warned.

Ginever grimaced.

"I suppose things have got a bit balled-up while I've been away," he admitted.

"They could be worse—but not much. I've stalled Cator, who was out for your blood; you let them down pretty badly over that last instalment of the serial. There may yet be a bit of trouble there; I played up your operation for all it was worth, but you know as well as I do, Cator's not responsive to sweet talk. There's also," said Harry, shuffling papers on his desk, "a nasty sharp edge to the last notice from the Inland Revenue; I've had Mackintosh on the blower every ten minutes over the last six weeks. He wants to know if they're your accountants or if they're your accountants."

"That's Ann's end!"

"Ann's a grand girl, but there's a human limit. Why in

77

hell," asked Harry amiably, "can't you answer a letter now and again?"

Ginever whistled a few bars of "Christians awake, salute this happy morn," and Harry smiled grudgingly, lowering his tortoise-like eyelids and lighting another cigar; taking his time.

"I'm only making sure you'll lunch with me tomorrow. The office opens on Wednesday, and I'd like to have a few things cut and dried." He refilled Ginever's glass. "And how about the book?" he enquired.

That was getting on, Ginever told him untruthfully.

"You gave them June as the deadline, didn't you?"

Ginever said that, so far as his novels were concerned, he did not admit any deadline; the book was finished, or it wasn't, and the only person to say when it was finished was himself, George Ginever. Harry nodded understandingly; he had sufficient experience of the vagaries of authors not to turn the steam on. At the same time, he had some degree of sympathy for publishers, who had to compile their lists against a background of printers' strikes and rising costs.

"The Ellises want to let their villa at Antibes through February and early March. He's going to get a book in West Africa. Why don't you take the villa over? Big studio, five or six rooms, all mod. con. I stayed there last year. Good place for work, you could finish the first draft of the novel and lick it into shape in time to get it into the autumn lists, and then you can concentrate on that *Women's World* assignment that comes up in May—"

Ginever, a man of moderate speech, swore explicitly and obscenely at the *Women's World* and at editors in general. Harry lifted an eyebrow and lit another cigar.

"All right; you can have it. I've chucked the novel."

"That'll be news for Peter. You've had a couple of thousand advance, haven't you?"

"All right; I'll send them a cheque. And you can tell *Women's World* where to put themselves."

"Well." Harry scratched the back of his neck. "So far that's about fifteen thousand down the drain. And the next thing?" he enquired ironically.

"Well: I'm going to try and write a book. I mean, a real book."

"Film in it?" came cautiously from Harry.

"No." He snapped his lips on it.

"I—see. Uh-huh. And what's your wife say to this?"

"Blythe? I haven't said anything to her about it. As a matter of fact, I've come back to ask Blythe for a divorce."

"And what does she say to that?" Nothing could shake Harry's imperturbability.

"Dammit, I haven't been back twenty-four hours—and divorce isn't the kind of thing you drop on Christmas morning!"

Harry's tortoise-lidded glance was a negation of all the Christmas sentiments. His only interest in the private affairs of his clients was the effect they might have on the work. But —so far as he was capable of being fond—he had a kind of fondness for his client, George Ginever. And he had always detested Ginever's wife, for no particular reason. He had a warm dislike of women in general, and particularly of driving women: of whom Blythe Ginever was the worst example he remembered over years. But they—he and she—had worked together to establish Ginever and this . . . Harry pursed his lips and absently whistled a phrase.

"What's that?"

"*You* wouldn't know," said Harry rudely. "Gershwin and Cole Porter are more in your line. It happens to be Gilbert and Sullivan—'O, the doing and undoing—'"

He found himself telling Harry about Luce.

"We met at rehearsals. She's got a place on Long Island she rents from her husband's mother—"

79

"Married?" said Harry tiredly. He was used, on behalf of his clients, to sorting out this kind of mess, but had not, so far been called in to the rescue of Ginever.

"He was killed in a plane crash . . . One way or another we saw a lot of each other. After I was sick in New York she got me over to some friends of hers at Hyannis. I was trying to work, and that was too social. So she proposed I should take over her cottage at Oyster Bay. She was still understudying, and it was more convenient for her to share a flat with a girl in the Village. They came down weekends. Well," he ended lamely, "that was that."

"And now you want your wife to divorce you."

"It's the reasonable thing, isn't it? She's had no good out of me for years. She should be as glad of her freedom as I."

"Freedom. A beautiful word. A beautiful, beautiful thought." Harry tapped the ash of his cigar. "More or less obsolete . . . Well: she's got plenty to lose. Has she anything in particular to gain?"

"You're a bloody old cynic, Harry," said Ginever good-temperedly, "and you're a lucky bastard, because you've managed down the ages, to avoid emotional ties. You've never been in love with a man or a woman, have you? Now, have you?"

"Yes; I've been passionately in love with myself.— Now, look here, George: suppose your wife won't play. Where do we go from there?"

"I don't know. I simply don't know. Except—somehow or other—I've got to try and get free. So far as my work's concerned, it's possibly too late. Let's pretend it isn't. Let's pretend it's possible to recapture the first, fine, careless rapture! I know—and you know—it isn't. But, by God, Harry, I've bought my freedom and you know it. I've paid off my owings. Blythe's had what she wanted out of me—and now—and now—"

"Yes: and now?" said Harry, as he stammered into silence.

"Do you imagine, after what you've been doing, you're going to work back to your *Goose* and your *Fox?* Come off it.— It might interest you to know that between the wars I wrote some goodish poems that got into some of the anthologies. No, they weren't signed Harry Lasker; I called myself something else. I couldn't write a line of them today. You can't set the clock back.— Anyhow: what the hell's this got to do with getting rid of your wife?"

Ginever glanced at his watch.

"More than I've got time to tell you at present. But I believe it will all work out, if we all behave in a civilised manner."

"Sure," said Harry, with limitless irony. "If you all act big—you, and your wife, and your Miss—pardon me, Mrs.— van Thal. Not knowing *her*, can't give an opinion."

"You can take my opinion," said Ginever stiltedly.

Harry made a mock-respectful gesture.

"Granted. It hasn't, I suppose, escaped your attention that Mrs. Ginever is going to require some powerful inducement to let go?" He paused. "Money—we can include that out. So what?"

It was not for him to reveal Blythe's private affairs to Harry Lasker, for the present.

"Well, there's time enough for that . . . My preoccupation, just now, is Fla.— It's all right, you don't have to crawl back into your shell; I'm not going to bore you with my domestic life."

"Good. I never majored in domesticity."

"That kid is important—to both of us."

"Meaning—?" For the first time Harry's eyes opened wide.

"No, no—a thousand noes. Fla's not going to be made a bargaining point. What I mean is—Fla hasn't got to suffer in this business, if it can be helped. So—I've got to play this pretty: do you see?"

"Quite. And, in the meanwhile, if it were not rude to ask

—what about your work? Do you really mean you are packing up the Cator contract, the *Women's World*—and Peter Finch, who's given you a very good deal over the last few years? — I suppose you know both Cator and *Women's World* could sue you for breach?"

"They could, but they won't," said Ginever shrewdly. "I'm sorry, Harry; you've done a marvellous job for me. I read a few of my letters this morning; I've seen some of the stuff you've got lined up. You're a hell of a fine agent, and believe me, I'm grateful for everything. But I'm going for fifty, and it's time you—and some other people—let me live my own life. Forgive me, Harry, but the pair of you have had your whack out of me. I mean, you and my wife.

"I *must* start over again. You may be right: there may be nothing left to start with. That remains to be seen. I must try and do something—before it's too late. There's no need for us —you and me—to make speeches. But will you please grasp that I'm in earnest about this—?"

"Even my limited intelligence," said Harry Lasker, "has taken me as far as that; it's somewhat—disconcerting. It rather reminds me of a friend of mine—a convinced (so it seemed to me) agnostic—who got religion—"

"By God, you've got something there, Harry.— What happened to him—your friend?" asked Ginever curiously.

"He took a bottleful of Nembutal," was the brief reply.

"Uh-huh. Well, apart from not having the slightest inclination, I'd never have the guts to kill myself; you can put that on the record. If I'm ever found dead in what might be described as suspicious circumstances, you can take it for granted it's natural causes."

Harry muttered something under his breath.

"What's that you said?" asked Ginever politely.

"I said, 'If it's not murder.'— Look: you're an efficient writer, you're a first-class craftsman, and you've got a very good reputation in the business. Can't you for God's sake be satisfied with what you've got?— Wait for it—" as Ginever was about to speak. "I don't share your inhibitions," sneered Harry, "about bringing up unpleasant subjects on Christmas morning! Have you, by any chance—if it were not rude to ask—a notion at the back of your mind that you're a frustrated genius?"

"Don't be such a blistering fool, Harry! I'm not going to be provoked into a row."

"Row me no rows. Favour me with a straight answer to a simple question."

"I knew exactly how much I owe you and, let's face it, my wife. I was a high-flying young author with delusions of grandeur. You both recognized I hadn't got what it takes . . . so, between you, you made me into something successful . . . All right; I've had that, I know the smell and the taste of what's called 'success.' I've gone off it—like you go off oysters, or *foie gras*, if you have too much of it. I just want to—"

"Yes?" prompted Harry.

Ginever gave rather a sheepish smile. He got up and dropped his hand on Harry's shoulder.

"Never mind, old boy; you wouldn't understand if I told you. So—till tomorrow? Where? What time?"

They fixed it and Harry sulkily jotted something down on his pad, and sullenly let Ginever out the front door.

He was more disturbed than he professed to be. His emotions—a word which, applied to Harry Lasker, would have raised a guffaw wherever two or three of his customers were gathered together—were analogous to those of a parent who, having backed a favourite son, is suddenly let down.

What the hell kind of a woman had he found this time? He was obviously floating on a blue cloud—and it was going to be about as easy to get rid of that wife of his as to prise a barnacle off a rock with a silver teaspoon. For once, Harry Lasker found himself on Blythe's side: at any rate, until he had had a look at the woman.

83

Chapter Six

Walking home across the Park, Ginever thought of Christmas at Oyster Bay; of the carol party Luce had worked up for a bunch of kids and the crèche he had helped her prepare, with a procession of little santons she had brought back from a visit to Provence. "That's your candle," she said, putting it at the feet of the Babe. All that long way away, "his" candle was burning; by now, surely, it would have burnt out. "Someday," said Luce, with her sweet, wide smile, "we'll have Christmas together. We'll get up early and go to church—'When shepherds watched,' and all that lot. It's the one day in the year when I feel like church. When we were kids, and Dad had his assignment in Spain, we went to a midnight mass. I can't think why; they were Methodists, if anything, my parents. But I don't think they ever took religion—the formalized sort—seriously; they were just decent Christians. There was a dance at the hotel and just before midnight all the Catholics went across the Square to the church—the women with pieces of black lace over their heads. Carola and I went along; she was fifteen and I was a kid of eleven. I'd never felt Christmas like I felt it that night, kneeling on those stone-cold flags, and the candles, and the music, and coming out afterwards and the sky all bristling with stars . . . it was the first time I'd come up against the magical, mystical feeling of Christmas."

Entering the drawing room, he received Lady Adela's dried-flower-like kiss and the shrivelled handshake of his father-in-law. Two young men—introduced as Peter and Colin—and a young woman—introduced as Lily Brawne—made him kindly welcome; Colin gave him an ashen smile and offered him his own sherry. "So heavenly of you to have us; Christmas is just too, too grue, isn't it, with no domestics or anything."

"Brawne? Lovely old English name," Lady Adela was murmuring. "Fanny, you know." She adjusted her deaf-aid. "I didn't quite catch: is it the Norfolk Brawnes or the Shropshire lot?"

"It's the Mile End Road lot," shouted Miss Brawne. "My mother was an office cleaner: Elsie Brawne. And who my father was I haven't a clue, and neither has she!"

"Lily's so snob," cooed the one called Peter. "After all, we can't all be bastards, darling!"

"No, no," said Lady Adela enthusiastically. "Now do tell me, Miss Brawne . . ."

The Master—Ginever inevitably thought of him as the Master, although Professor Cherrill had been retired four years—gave his son-in-law a dimly affectionate look as the latter joined him, glass in hand.

"Well, my boy. Glad you got back for 'the festive season.' 'Life still hath one romance that naught can bury.'"

"'For still will Christmas gild the year's mischances,'" he capped the quotation, and caught the appreciative twinkle in the Master's eye.

"Ha; so you know it. Limited fellow, very, but he struck out the occasional note.— I don't know these people, do you?" the Master shouted confidentially; he had got in the habit of shouting to his wife. Ginever shook his head. "Friends of Blythe's, I suppose. D'you know what I miss. An old-fashioned panto. Malcolm Scott. Wilkie Bard. You're too young to have known 'em. 'I'd like to sing in op'ra,'" crooned the Master.

"I'm sorry, darling," Blythe was screaming behind him, "but I hate that purple stuff you're putting in Oggie's music room. Well, I've just got a thing against purple—even if you call it violet."

So he said. So she said. Seven voices, seven minds in discord. And where, he wondered, was Flavia?

The telephone rang as they were finishing their drinks.

"All right; I'll take it upstairs," said Ginever, as Blythe was moving to lift the receiver. "It's for me—New York."

"George—please! Lunch is just coming up!"

"Very well; don't wait."

Luce's voice came through as clear as though she were in the next room.

"Merry Christmas. What was the trip like?"

"Pure hell. Is that you?" he said inanely.

"Yeah, it's me." He heard her deep chuckle. "Listen, darling: I've got some news for you."

"Good news?"

"Sure. I wouldn't give you anything else, would I, on Christmas Day? When we've got over the New Year, Belle-mère's going to recuperate in Quebec, with her family."

"So—?"

"So don't you see? I can nip over to Europe for a day or three. I can't say positively when: it will depend on her and you know what she is about changing plans. I'll ring or cable. And—darling—don't ring again until you hear from me. Write. Write every day—if you can."

"I'll write every day. You've made my Christmas." Dreams surely went by contraries . . .

When he came out of the office, Blythe and Flavia were on the landing below.

"—might have the common courtesy to ring up!" Blythe was saying.

" 'Common courtesy!' Really, Mummy, how corny can you get!" scornfully, from Flavia.

"Manners are not corny, my dear child." With exaggerated patience. "I thought we'd agreed on that."

"It's your fault; I told you not to ask him."

"And he accepted."

"What did you expect him to do? Shout No and stamp out, slamming the door?"

"That sounds more in character."

"It was so silly of you. I've asked you before not to interfere with my friends."

"All right; I made a mistake. I only thought"—her voice was unsteady—"it would be jollier for you to have somebody of your own age—and you could have gone upstairs afterwards and amused yourselves in your own way—"

"Will you please leave me to give my own invitations in future?" said Flavia icily.

Their voices faded away down the stairs.

The conversation round the luncheon table reached an all-time low. What, wondered Ginever, had possessed Blythe, that admirable hostess, to get together this bunch of uncongenial people for Christmas luncheon? He found himself throwing glances of sympathy at Flavia, who wore a bright, polite smile and was attentive to her grandparents. He had exhausted his travel talk. Blythe herself barely troubled to conceal her boredom—though the two young men were wildly gay, their gaiety taking the form of ragging Miss Brawne who, smouldering through her turkey, did not pretend to be enjoying her meal or her company. The Master, that delightful conversationalist, repository of the wit and humour of half a century, barely uttered; Lady Adela, her deaf-aid abandoned, was having too much difficulty with her new dentures to bestow more than an absent smile or nod to left or right. Stupefied, Ginever listened to himself making inane remarks—to which nobody paid any attention. When at last Blythe rose from a litter of nutshells and said in a dying voice, "We'll have coffee upstairs, shall we?" and there was a shuffling of chairs and dropping of napkins, he felt like one partly drowned, cast up by a sluggish tide on a mud flat.

Finding himself for a moment alone with Flavia, he stared at her glassily, and she gave a ghostly giggle.

"What are they? Who are they?" He had had a little too much wine. Flavia giggled again, more faintly.

"It was a bit of a mess-up," she admitted. "It wasn't Mummy's fault, really," she said, on the note of one determined, against her inclinations, to be fair. "After all, we didn't know until last Thursday that you'd be back for Christmas." That was true enough. "And it was fixed up that we were going to lunch with the Grans."

"I seem to have caused a great deal of inconvenience," said Ginever, sounding to himself detestably tetchy. "Was there any particular reason why I shouldn't have been welcome at the Grans'?"

"Oh, Daddy, of course not! But you know Gramma. As soon as she heard you were coming home she went into a blind flap. They're staying at rather a tatty hotel this time, because Grappa's doing some research and has to be close to the Museum. Oh dear," said Flavia, imitating her grandmother, "it wouldn't do at all to have dear George to Christmas lunch in so dull a place, with a lot of stuffy old people! So Mummy said, it was a bit late, but she'd try to get a table for five at the Caprice—and then Grappa dug his toes in." Her giggles by now were nearly hysterical. "You know how he abominates smart, social places. So he said he would go off and lunch at the Athenaeum, and of course that sent Gramma up in the air. Surely Mummy could get together a delightful little party of nice, interesting people to welcome you home! So," said Flavia, a trifle grimly, "Ann and Ma spent forty-eight hours, ringing up what Gramma calls 'nice, interesting people' and of course they were all dated up: who isn't, over Christmas?"

Who indeed?

"I still don't see why we couldn't have eaten our turkey and pud peacefully here—just ourselves and the Grans."

Flavia shook her head.

"Gramma's not domestic—you know that; and she gets so terribly fed up with Boar's Hill, and when she comes to town she wants to make it one long riot. They came up ten days ago, and she hasn't had any fun and she was positively weepy about Christmas Day. It was wild joy to know you were coming home! It meant being taken places and meeting people—and when Mummy told her we couldn't find anybody for lunch, and it would just be a family affair, she blenched. Yes, positively, she blenched. Couldn't Mummy find some young people, some gay people—never mind if they weren't particularly famous. Sweet old harpy," said Flavia affectionately; she was fond of her grandmother. "She was set on making you an excuse for a party! They could just as well have had one themselves and invited us, but Grappa's gone a bit mean; he's been spending an awful lot on hothouses and experiments with composts, and Gramma's bored sick. She's really *enjoyed* this grisly lunch!" She broke off with a sigh. "I'm sorry. Anyhow—I'm going out. Isn't Christmas frightful?" she exploded, as she rushed from the room.

"It's been quite, quite delightful," Lady Adela was saying, when he joined them upstairs. "Those amusing boys and that entertaining Miss Brawne! So nice to hear that good old English word bastard. You must take me to her play; those boys say it's kitchen sink. We're all involved with sinks nowadays, aren't we?— Are you ready, dear?" she asked the Master.

While they were seeing the old Cherrills into a taxi, the telephone started to ring. He left Blythe to look after her parents and picked up the dining-room extension.

An unfamiliar voice asked:

"Can I speak to Mrs. Ginever?"

"She's engaged. Can I take a message? I'm her husband."

"Oh . . . I'm terribly sorry to trouble you. I'm Mrs. Dawlish. Is my son there?"

"We've had a luncheon party but everybody's gone. Would it be Peter?—or Colin?"

"No; Gerald," said Mrs. Dawlish faintly. "I'm so sorry to be a nuisance. Could I speak to Flavia?"

"She went out about an hour ago, but we're expecting her in this evening. Would you like me to leave a message, or anything?"— It was evident that Mrs. Dawlish, whoever she might be, was in distress.

"Oh, that would be so kind! Please ask her to ring me when she comes in."

"I certainly will. Would she know the number?"

"Bayswater 0071. I'd better explain—we're rather worried. Gerald hasn't been home since yesterday. It may be a fuss about nothing—but you know what they are! They go off, and we're expected to take it in our stride—but—with all the things that happen on the roads at holiday times—!"

"If it was anything of that kind I think you'd have heard." He tried to sound consoling.

"That's what my husband says. But they do such idiotic things—get themselves into trouble—"

"Is Flavia a particular friend of your son's?" asked Ginever cautiously.

"I really don't know. But I rang a boy who used to come round here—thinking Gerald might be with him—and he happened to give me Flavia's name. It's just a matter of leaving no stone unturned!"

"I'll certainly tell her to ring you up. Gerald Dawlish," he repeated unnecessarily.

"She probably calls him Bull; they all have silly names!"

"Hold on a minute. Bull—yes; he came last night, I think it would be between seven and eight. I was in by myself so I went to the door."

"Oh! Did he—what did he say?"

91

"I asked him in but he wouldn't come. He left a parcel for my daughter. If you hold on," said Ginever after a pause, "I might be able to find it. There might be a message or something inside." The poor woman was in such distress, it seemed the least he could do.

"Please do try and find it," she begged.

Where to look? It had gone from the hall, and if Flavia had opened it there would most likely be nothing but a crumple of brown paper, indistinguishable from other wrappings—except that most people nowadays did gift parcels up in decorative papers.

He ran up to the attic room, and almost the first thing his eyes lit on was the packet, lying unopened in the middle of the floor. A pair of stiletto heels had mashed it. Inside the punctured paper he felt, as he had guessed, a record. He pulled out the scarred disc. There was no other enclosure.

"I found it. I'm sorry, there's no message. It's a gramophone record, called—just a minute, the label's got scratched —it looks like 'Get with It': does that convey anything?"

"Not a thing. Well—thank you for taking so much trouble."

"I'll see that Flavia rings you as soon as she comes in. If there's anything else I can do, let me know, will you."

"It's so very kind of you. My husband wants to ring the police, but I think that's a last recourse, don't you? Gerald would be furious. He'll probably walk in at any minute and call us fools for making a fuss!" she concluded, trying to make light of it.

Blythe's door was shut; she was no doubt having a rest before her evening party. The servants hired for the luncheon had cleared up and cleared out. He left his own door open and read letters, until he heard the gentle slam downstairs.

"Hi!" he called, as Flavia flashed across the landing.

"Oh—hi!" She hovered uncertainly on the threshold.

"Mrs. Dawlish wants you to ring her up."

"Mrs.— *Who*? Oh. What for?" She sounded startled and wary.

"You can take the call here." He pointed to the telephone.

"Oh, I won't disturb you, Daddy. I'll take it in the drawing room," she muttered, and was swinging away when he recalled her.

"Do me the favour to take that call in here."

Their eyes met, and hers narrowed at the note of authority.

"I'm sure I don't know what this is in aid of," she bluffed. Ginever steeled himself.

"Will you for once do as you're asked without making an issue of it?" (And suppose I don't win? he asked himself.)

She scowled, bit her lip, but, after a brief hesitation, lifted the receiver. He noticed she dialled the number without prompting.

"This is Flavia.— No, Mrs. Dawlish. As a matter of fact I haven't seen him for ages.— Well, since Friday.— Well, he was asked to lunch, but he didn't come.— No, really, I don't know.— Well, I'm sorry, but that's how it is.— No, I don't know anything about his plans, or—or anything! I don't see why you're asking me.— Oh, I expect he's with some of his friends and he'll turn up sometime. What did you say? Oh— thank you; and happy Christmas to *you*. Well—goodnight."

"Flavia!"

She swung round, on the defensive.

"What's all this about?"

"I haven't a clue," she shrugged.

"You asked him to luncheon today."

"I did *not!*" she said with indignation. "It was Mummy," she muttered.

"Well, what for? I mean, is he one of your regular dates?" Knowing it was irritating her, Ginever plugged on. If there was trouble in the air—and, by the pricking of his thumbs, there seemed to be—he did not want Flavia involved in it.

"Oh, Daddy, don't be such a square! He's just one of the gang."

"Sit down. Have a cigarette"—he pushed the box towards her.

"Thank you, I don't smoke," said Flavia, but sat down. He felt her young toleration reaching towards him as he lit his own cigarette, and prayed inwardly that some celestial power would help him not to bungle this situation. It did not seem credible that six months' absence had cut this gulf between himself and his daughter.

"Go on; tell us about the 'gang.'"

"We have parties upstairs; Coke and bangers and TV and talk; mostly talk. So what? Isn't that what my room's for?"

"Of course it's what your room's for," he said, on what he hoped was not too placatory a note. "I just happened to wonder what made your mother invite this particular member of the gang—who appears to have a perfectly good home and family of his own—to lunch on Christmas Day."

"Don't ask *me*. But I don't see why I've got to be put through this Third Degree stuff, because I happen to be—to be *acquainted* with Bull Dawlish!" she brought out on a stammer.

"Honey, there's no Third Degree. But if this chap has got himself into any kind of trouble, I'd rather you weren't associated with it."

"But I'm *not!*" said Flavia violently. "Look, it's like this; Mummy loathes most of the gang, but Bull gets past because he happens to be public school and all that jazz! He has all the answers—her sort of answers," she said with scorn. "I suppose," she said, off at a tangent, "I suppose you call it reasonable, that I'm not allowed to have a latchkey."

"What do you call it?" he teased her, and was relieved to see her taut little face relax into rather a watery grin.

"Oh, I know. All the same, it's a bit shaming. I mean, when I bring friends home, and Mummy opens the door and does

94

'the gracious hostess'! And when I've got a party, and she comes upstairs and jollies us as if we're kids in the nursery. She always brings up a gorgeous cake, or sandwiches, or something, but—you know: she expects to be introduced, and the whole thing goes cockeyed—the gang, my friends, just aren't like that, and it makes me feel a perfect clot, and—and I wonder"—her voice trembled—"whether they'll ever come again."

He wondered if, and doubted that, Lausanne would resolve all this.

"Now—to get back to this Bull character—"

Flavia heaved a sigh of exaggerated patience.

"Don't you *see?* Mummy asked Bull to lunch so that I should have somebody of my own age at the grown-up party! I begged and implored her not to, but you know what she's like when she gets an idea into her head. He was as petrified as I was—so he said Yes—and I wouldn't be surprised," she mumbled, "if that's why he bolted."

"That was a bit exaggerated, wasn't it? I mean, he could simply have stayed away, instead of putting his parents to all this worry," said Ginever mildly. She shrugged her shoulders, looking out of the corners of her eyes. She knows something, he thought, and she's not fool enough to think I'm taken in by this cock-and-bull story; she just doesn't mean to tell. "After all, it's Christmas—"

"And all that!" burst out Flavia. "The way you go on, all of you, about Christmas! 'Peace on earth, goodwill to men!' I suppose they're singing that at Aldermaston, and—and in American churches where they won't let black people kneel down in company with whites? What's Christmas, except an excuse for making a pig of yourself and spending a lot of money in having yourself a good time? Mummy—with her Christmas lunch for people who 'have nowhere to go'!" she went on incoherently. "And there wasn't one person round that table who couldn't have taken himself to lunch at the

95

Savoy—and hundreds and thousands perishing with cold and aching with homesickness, round the Portobello Road—"

He felt inclined to say that the people of whom Flavia was evidently thinking would have ached no less round the dining-room table; that they were undoubtedly happier, aching in each others' company, than they would have been, transported into a foreign milieu; but realised it was not the moment for levity. Moreover, he found himself with her over the "Peace on earth" slogan, than which none more hollow now echoed over so-called Christian earth.

"Look. I took the trouble to cross the Atlantic, to be with you at Christmas. I didn't come to make a pig of myself, or to spend money; I could have done both, effectively, in New York. So—what's Christmas?"

"Oh, Daddy!" She burst into tears.

My poor, unhappy, little girl, thought Ginever, as he held her. And— What the hell have we been up to, Blythe and I, to produce this?

Presently she pulled herself out of his arms.

"I must go and get dressed for the party. Sorry, Daddy, I love you—and I didn't mean that about Christmas."

"And I love you.— Hi!" he called her back from the door. "I've got a confession to make. While you were out I went up to your room."

Instantly suspicious—"What for?" she asked.

"I went to look for that parcel you had from Bull. I found it—you know where. I'm not asking you anything, I'm telling you. I opened it—what there was left to open."

"You opened my private parcel." She drew an incredulous breath. "It's the sort of thing Mummy might do; but you—!"

"Listen: can't you see that when a person's missing it's a pretty serious thing?"

"Missing!" she said scornfully. "Bull goes off somewhere, because he just happens to want to, and you say he's 'missing'! —as if he was a kid who'd got lost on his way to the pub. He probably went off to dodge Christmas in the bosom of the family." She was twisting the buckle of her belt frantically. "Anyhow, what's that got to do with opening my parcel?" she demanded.

"His mother thought there might be something in it that would give them a clue. Goddammit," exploded Ginever, "how d'you think we'd feel, if you vanished into the night?"

"I'm a girl—and I'm only fifteen," said Flavia feebly, and waited. "Well: was there anything?" He felt she was frightened of the reply.

"No, there wasn't. Here's the remains, if you want them." He held out the mess of paper and the disc to her; she snatched them and slammed them into the waste-paper bin.

"You're welcome!— You wouldn't have dared to do that if —if I was grown-up!" she sobbed, and rushed from the room.

She was right; he would have waited until she came in, and spoken to her about it. But—that poor, demented woman on the telephone: to give her some sort of assurance seemed the immediate thing.

Chapter Seven

On Boxing Day the telephone never stopped ringing; the news of his return had got around—presumably through Harry Lasker. There were invitations for himself and Blythe, for himself alone, for all three of them. He kept his luncheon date with Harry—which was not convivial; Harry had been strictly accurate in saying that his affairs could be in worse condition, but not much. There were obviously strenuous weeks ahead. He entered some dates into his diary, with the private proviso that, if Luce arrived, he would cut any one of them, if only for twenty-four hours. He tried, for the time being, to put Luce to the back of his mind: ridiculous effort! Luce occupied the front, the middle, the back, every minutest corner and pocket of his mind. Life without Luce was an aching emptiness. He had never known anything quite like that emptiness. It both thrilled and shocked him; rendered him stronger and more vulnerable. Because of his love for Luce he found himself capable of a consideration, even a gentleness, towards other people of which he had never imagined himself capable. He could be patient and courteous with people who irritated him, or he even actively disliked. It could not possibly last, of course: this curiously elevated state of mind!—which rather reminded him of his boyhood, and the exaltation—lasting only a few hours—after receiving the Sacrament in the School Chapel.

On the following day he proposed taking Blythe and Flavia out to lunch. Blythe said she had planned the day in bed and Flavia, at one o'clock, had not yet had her bath. So he lunched at the Savile, played a game of snooker, and got home between five and six—to find both of them out. Towards seven the telephone rang, and it was Mrs. Dawlish.

"I thought you might care to know: we've heard from Gerald."

"Good show. So he's all right."

"Let's hope so! He wired us from Newhaven—and his passport's gone. Aren't they *awful?*" she chattered. "Never occurs to them that we worry. Not a word of plans—no address! So far as we know, he might have taken off for the moon."

"Not from Newhaven. You'll probably have news from Dieppe," said Ginever, and hung up. A nice, silly woman; he felt sorry for her, as one who had not yet managed to adjust to the contemporary design for living.

The telephone rang again, and the voice of one of his best friends invited him and Blythe to supper. He said Blythe was out, and proposed another date. The next ring was from Flavia.

"I've been asked to a party, Daddy, but I won't go if you're by yourself."

He said, rather stiffly, that he had a date, but presumed he might see her in the morning. She said, "Oh, rather!" and, before he could add any more, said, "Okay then; cheer-O, Daddy-O!" and rang off, leaving him gaping at the receiver.

"Well, I'll be damned," he said aloud, and replaced it very quietly, as was his habit when he felt like slamming it down. He told himself that he was imagining the relief in Flavia's voice—and knew he was not; and told himself that it was perfectly natural that she should prefer her party to sitting around at home with him, and that it was unreasonable to feel hurt and annoyed—and went on being hurt and annoyed. And with his sacrosanct mood effectively destroyed—at any rate for the time being—he proceeded to ring up about twenty people and made engagements for the remainder of the week; he could cancel, if Flavia saw fit to give him any of her valuable time. In which mood of petulance he put on his coat and was about to return to the club.

Opening the door, however, he found Blythe on the step, fumbling for her key. She lifted her startled face, and he saw on it for a moment the illuminated look it had worn on the night of his return, the brilliant, contented look that no one who has loved can ever mistake; then it was gone, like the extinguished flame of a candle.

"Oh: are you going out for dinner?"

"I was," he said, and thought, Dam', I've spoiled something for her. This is the moment, he thought, when we ought to have it out: simply and candidly and without bitterness on either side, making it easy for each other. He found himself being fond of and even tender about her; he could, in that moment, have put his arms round her and said, "My dear, I know. I'm very glad, for both our sakes." Then, as he stood back to let her come in, as she brushed him with her furs, he caught that scent again and the impulse to tenderness was rebuffed; why had she had to lie to him about so trivial a thing? It was stupid, on his part, to care, but there it was: the mood which was on him was temporarily extinguished—like the flame in Blythe's face. On her face now was the expression of a disappointed child, robbed of a treat.

"So I needn't have come home after all," she pouted.

"Fla rang up just now; she's gone to a party. I didn't know whether you were coming in or not," he said coolly. "There doesn't appear to be anybody in the house."

"I ordered dinner for half past eight and said they could stay out until seven; if they aren't in they ought to be," frowned Blythe, reaching towards the bell, and checking as sounds came up from the basement. "Of course they're in; that's their wireless. So what do you want to do? I mean, are you going out or staying in? There's no point in cooking a meal if you're out—"

"Naturally I'm in if you are."

"I meant to ask you what your plans were for this evening, but before I got round to it you'd gone out. I took it for granted you'd leave me a note or something if you weren't coming in for dinner—"

"Look: let's go out," he interrupted. The prospect of dinner *tête-à-tête*, with Blythe nursing a grievance and disgruntled service casting gloom across the table, was not to be borne. "Let's go and have dinner at the Moulin, or somewhere. For God's sake let them go home—and tomorrow Ann will be back and she'll get me properly organised!"

She began by protesting that it was impossible—that the servants would never stand for being messed about like this, and where would they be if Mrs. Roberts gave notice, she had been on the verge for some time—and ended by saying she would go downstairs and *see*. As her heels tapped down the basement he went into the dining room and poured himself a Scotch. It was plain enough that, under all her protestations, Blythe was as relieved as he was that they were not dining by themselves—and equally plain that tonight was not the moment for the show-down—which would have to be forced within the next few days, in fairness to Luce, waiting for news on Long Island.

So they went out to dinner. An atmosphere of post-Christmas exhaustion hung over personnel and clientele alike: poached-egg eyes of men and slightly disordered coiffures of women who had not yet found time, or perhaps energy, to visit their hairdressers accompanied strangled yawns and indifference to the menu. The place, normally packed, was half empty, the dance band played, more or less in its sleep, to an empty floor. Missing the inexhaustible vivacity of New York, he felt apologetic to Blythe for bringing her out to so dull a place, and exerted himself to entertain her; and she, after a few doubtful moments and some glances of surprise, played up to him admirably. They succeeded, in fact, so well in their comedy of manners that they found themselves attracting some bleary attention from neighbouring tables. He had forgotten the pleasant—if in the circumstances somewhat artificial—sound of Blythe's laughter, and she—

"You know, George, I'd forgotten you could be such fun! New York's good for you; you ought to take more of it." She lifted her glass and flickered her eyelashes at him across it, reminding him of her mother. Not since they were engaged to be married did he remember her so gay, so oncoming! Granted it was, on both their parts, an "act"—Blythe, during his absence, had taken some good lessons in acting! The subdued lighting robbed her of years and the awareness of an audience kindled in her an animation that made her younger still. She had always, of course, been at her best with an audience. And he did not object to one himself. It would have been very different if they had been sitting opposite each other at the Queen Anne dining table, with one of the maidservants moving sullenly behind them, and not a sound but a car revving up outside and, at the opening of a door, the distant wireless. Boredom merging into a formless antagonism and eventually into that which above all he detested—bickering.

For years, he thought, they had needed a stage to put them at ease with each other. Absurd as it sounded, they could be fond—but genuinely fond—of each other in public; so much so that the Ginevers had something of a reputation for being a devoted couple! She, it was said, "put up with" his romantic vagrancies, because she knew his true devotion was to her. You only had to see the pair of them together, to know how perfectly they fitted. She, of course, was a good deal older, but Ginever was the kind who needed a maternal element in his marital relationship. It was easy enough to invent the gossip that idly looped itself round the marriage of George and Blythe Ginever. A couple at an adjoining table were looking at them, he thought, enviously.

He ought, Ginever considered, to have been offended: but he was not. Only amused, and glad to have given Blythe pleasure, and glad to have had pleasure from her. By tacit consent, not a word was said by either about Flavia. It was too evident that Flavia, on Blythe's side, was a touchy subject—and all *that* would eventually have to be gone into; but, for one evening at least they could avoid argument and partisanship and mutual reproaches—and perhaps that one evening might go into the balance against the trouble which was to come.

Kissing her goodnight, he said:

"Thank you very much for a delightful evening."

"I've enjoyed it too." The note of surprise in her voice nearly brought a laugh from him, which her next words destroyed. "Nobody could say we aren't civilised, could they?" said Blythe, and closed her bedroom door.

Ann Maxton turned up in the morning, as neat, fresh, and efficient as ever. When the greetings were over, and they had skimmed the more vital parts of the correspondence—

"Do you think you could lay hands on those notes on the *Oráculo?*" he asked her. She looked surprised, as well she might; his Gracián research, which he had abandoned as he had abandoned many things, dated back five or six years.

"It'll take a few minutes. Would you like to sign that little lot while you're waiting?" She laid a neat sheaf of typing in front of him.

"*'Know how to put your troubles on someone else's shoulders; it is a very skilful device of rulers,'*" he reminded her, quoting from the Spanish. "There's no immediate hurry."

"Are we going to have another crack at Gracián?" She sounded doubtful.

"I don't know. I'm in an unsettled sort of mood—I'll tell you about it sometime. Meanwhile—I would like to have a glance at those notes, if you've got them handy."

"Of course." She still sounded hesitant.

"Oh, come on, Ann; what's biting you?"

"I'm afraid things have got into rather a muddle, while you've been away."

"So I gather from Harry Lasker. I gather it's my fault—for not answering letters! I got a good caning from him yesterday. According to Harry, I've done you wrawng!" he grimaced. " 'You don't know nothen' yet!' Anyhow, what's this got to do with Gracián?"

"I rather hoped we could get some of the stuff tidied up, before you go into a new book," said Ann unhappily. "I've told Sheila and Carol to stand by for a rush job on the novel—"

"What novel?"

"George!"

"There isn't any novel. I put it in the fire.— Ann dear; don't look so awful. We'll have a session and I'll explain it all. First things first. You might get on to those agents who deal with the Anchorage" (the house at Marlow) "and find out if they've got anything in the way of a flat or a studio with living accommodation on their books. Anywhere within reason."

Theirs not to reason why. She did it without turning a hair, jotting addresses down on her pad. How, he wondered, would he ever have got on without calm, quiet Ann, who, in the years she had been with them, had made herself not merely into an excellent secretary, but an acceptable member of the household. Blythe, who liked her very much, sometimes teased him about his dependence on Ann. "That's right; you retreat behind Ann—she's your buffer state!"—to which he could have retorted that it works both ways. He could have cited a number of occasions when Ann covered up for Blythe.

"I suppose you know she's in love with you?" said Blythe.

"Oh, balls," said Ginever rudely. "She's in love with that

105

chap she was engaged to, who got smashed up on the race track and fell in love with the nurse while he was in hospital. The pin-up boy! He married the nurse and then got himself in the headlines with a movie star or beauty queen or some such. Ann's a one-man woman—and she's made a life for herself out of working for us."

Watching her neat head bent towards the telephone, he reflected that the changes he was planning were going to affect Ann heavily.

The door burst open and Flavia shot in.

"So sorry to interrupt—Ann: it's only Wednesday, but I'm terribly short!"

It was evidently a known formula. Ann opened a drawer, took out a note, and handed it over. Ginever felt for his wallet and remembered that, apart from some small change, he had nothing but dollar bills; so he leaned over, tweaked another note out of Ann's cash drawer, and passed it to Flavia.

"There you are—a Christmas bonus."

"Oh—thanks very much. I can use it!" she assured him.

"Good. Let's use it this afternoon. I want to see that picture at the Curzon—I missed it in New York."

"I'd love to. But—but I've got to meet Mummy at the tailor's, for a fitting," she stammered.

"Oh, go on: put it off."

"I could, but you know Mummy's 'little book'—Medes and Persians, tablets of stone, and what have you!" She laughed nervously.

"Well, go and ask her."

"No. No, I'd better not, really. You know how she hates upsetting her plans. I'm sorry—I'd have loved it," stammered Flavia, and rushed out.

Nunca descomponarse: how did it go—?

Never be put out. Sensible people make a special point of never being put out. It is the mark of a true man and of

106

great nobility of soul, for it is always difficult to upset the magnanimous. The passions are the humours of the soul and any excess on their part entails a disordered judgment . . .

(He and Walton had argued over the word "entails." Ginever proposed "implies," Walton accepted it, and, by accident or design, omitted to alter it in the proofs.)

Really angry, this time, he could not live up to the doctrine of perfection laid down by Gracián. His anger was not with Flavia, but with Blythe, who had sent up word she was out for lunch but would telephone about tea-time. She had not yet gone out, and he was inclined to go down and have it straight out with her.

He moved over to the window, and there was a big Italian car pulled up in front of the door.

"Who's that?" he asked Ann, who was looking over her shoulder.

"Mrs. Schneider's; nice job, isn't it? Reminds me: there's a chit from Walford's. About turning in the Wolseley. You ought to get a decent price." She quoted the mileage.

"All right: cope," he told her absently. His eyes were on the square. Blythe, smothered in furs, came out, with Oggie Schneider, followed by Flavia, who waved her hand and pattered off, evidently refusing a lift. A chauffeur got down and opened the door, the two women got in and were muffled in rugs. A bare, jewelled hand reached out and covered a gloved hand. From his angle of observation, Ginever could not see which was which.

They lunched at Ann's club. He had told her to reserve a table at the Caprice, and at the last moment jibbed at the social-professional jazz, the inevitable encounters with the film crowd, theatre crowd, journalist crowd: he was not yet ready for all that.

There was nobody he knew at Ann's club and, better still, nobody who knew him. They got an alcove table and Ann, knowing his taste, ordered *soupe à l'oignon*—which reminded him of Luce, the onion-soup queen; she did it the way you got it on the Left Bank, in a deep bowl, with a thick crust, bubbly and freckled. Theirs came in soup plates, with a last-minute sprinkling of Parmesan. While they waited for their cutlets—

"When exactly is Fla supposed to go to Lausanne?" he asked.

Her nice, long fingers with palely varnished nails crumbled her roll.

"Well, she's got some sort of a tooth infection, and the dentist doesn't want her to go until it's cleared up. It may be all right. Of course, Fla hopes it won't. She'd sooner have every tooth in her head pulled out—I'm a little bit on her side," admitted Ann.

"Well: go on."

"It's a swing-over, isn't it, from that school in Kensington, and all the friendships she's made? I agree with Blythe, that they aren't, all of them, desirable. But the fact remains, she's made them, and they matter to her, and it's like tearing up her roots."

"I suppose that's our fault. We ought to have sent her to boarding school earlier."

"It might have been easier all round." She gave him a direct look. "Do give her as much of your time as you can; it might just tip the scale," she said urgently.

"How the hell do I give her my time, when she dodges every chance we've had, so far, of being together?" asked Ginever, with reason.

"At Flavia's age, six months is a long time. She feels 'out of touch.' And she's scared stiff over this boarding-school business."

"But why? Look here; we talked it over—the three of us—last year, at Marlow—"

"Nearly eighteen months ago," put in Ann.

"And she was as keen as mustard, about finishing her education abroad."

"Yes, and she's going a year earlier than she expected, and she's too young for the Sorbonne or Perugia. She accepts that."

"So what doesn't she accept?" he asked. "The discipline?"

"No." Ann shook her head. "That's what Blythe says. But it goes deeper than that. Fla feels that her status with her own age-group is at stake. Under their 'pop' and 'twist' and barnying around the coffee bars, a lot of them are quite serious, you know. And Fla feels this plush boarding school is going to cut her off from all the things her gang consider important."

"And what is this 'gang,' anyhow?"

Ann shrugged her shoulders.

"How should I know? I'm what they call a square, if not a museum piece, to that age-group. But Blythe's been marvellous about it—really marvellous. She did manage to put her foot down about the coffee bars and murky assignments in strange flats, and Flavia's taken it very well, on the whole. I think, in some ways, she actually prefers having her friends here." Ann laughed quietly. "I guess it's some sort of a status symbol, to have a room of your own, with TV and record player, not to mention food and heating laid on! Some of those kids—well, don't ask *me* how they live."

She said suddenly, "I hate being a sneak, but—there've been incidents."

The "incidents" came out, under pressure: disappearance of small portable objects from downstairs—a watch of Blythe's, cigarettes, the odd bottle of gin, a pair of fur-lined boots; small sums of money plundered from Blythe's handbag, which she was in the careless habit of leaving in the hall or the toilet.

"We knew it couldn't be the dailies; they've never been known to pinch so much as the butt-end of an old lipstick. Anyhow, they're too well paid to bother about our leavings! It was horribly tricky; we didn't dare mention it to Flavia, she would have gone round the bend. Blythe says some of the kids are East Enders; so they may be. Personally, I don't see any more morality so far as property is concerned in our young ones than in the Mile End Road lot. But you know how it is," she concluded. "'Equality's' the religion, and 'equality' means that the docks are always right and Mayfair or Tooting Bec or what-have-you always wrong. If we'd so much as hinted, Flavia was capable of sweeping out. That, at all costs, had to be avoided.

"Are you serious about this studio idea?" she asked presently.

"Yes, I am. There's got to be a reorganisation," he muttered. He would have liked to tell her about Luce, but for obvious reasons could not.

"It would make an enormous difference to the work," soberly said Ann.

"Yes; you're had a pretty tough time. Unnecessarily so," he conceded.

Ginever went to the Savile, where he found a BBC executive he had met on a number of occasions at Olga Schneider's. He suggested a series, and Ginever was non-committal, though the project was tempting. His companion indicated astonishment that anything—anything in the world—could stand up against a proposition from the BBC, and Ginever laughed good-humouredly and proposed a game of snooker, took a thorough beating, and ordered tea.

"I suppose you've heard about the divorce?"

"Which one?"

"Virginia's gone off to the South of France with Beryl Alton; that won't last. Oggie's incommunicado at Arlington Street. I'm supposed to be dining there on the twelfth; not a word from Oggie to say whether it's on or off," he prattled; sent his love to Blythe and, pleading an appointment with his dentist, departed. Which reminded Ginever that he had himself intended to have an overhaul, so he rang his own dentist to find out if there was any chance of an appointment within the next few days. He was asked to wait a moment, and Stan Wellcome himself came to the telephone.

"Hallo. I'd heard you were back. Come right round. No, I can't make it tomorrow, I'm off to Málaga at the weekend. If you can wait till I'm back—?"

The hall porter got him a taxi and he went on to Harley Street.

When Stan Wellcome had finished playing jingle-bells round his jaws and given him a polish-up, and they were having a glass of sherry, he asked:

"What's this infection of Flavia's?"

Stan looked at him blankly.

"Flavia? I haven't seen her for twelve months. No, perhaps since last Spring," he corrected himself. "What do you mean, 'infection'? She'd better come round tomorrow at lunch-time —can we pop her in?" he asked the secretary, who consulted the book. There was some inaudible mumbling, during which Ginever wondered what mare's-nest he was on to now. "Tell her five minutes past one, bang on."

When he got home he gave Flavia the message, and her eyes flickered; it was obvious she was taken aback.

"Look, honey," said her father quietly. "You don't want to go to Lausanne, and we'll have to talk about that. But you're not being driven into anything, and there's no point in making up fairy tales."

The crimson ran up her cheeks and into the roots of her hair. Taking pity on her embarrassment, he turned his back, and added, to cover her silence, "By the way, I suppose you know your friend's turned up."

"What friend?"

"The Dawlish lad."

"Oh, *him*. I don't see why I'm supposed to take all this interest in Bull Dawlish, Daddy."

So that's it, thought Ginever. There's been something there, and the poor kid considers she's let down. Her next words confirmed the impression.

"And might I ask *where*," said Flavia on a note of exaggerated indifference, "Bull Dawlish has turned up?"

"His mother says he wired them from Newhaven. As he seems to have taken his passport, it rather looks as if he's gone, or is trying to go, abroad. Has he got enough money for that?"

"Bull? He's got plenty of money!" she burst out, then, as if aware of having committed herself too far—"at least, so far as *I'm* aware. I don't know why I should be expected to know anything about his private affairs. And I couldn't care less!" she concluded, with the over-protestation of her age and sex. "I must go and change—oh my goodness, I nearly forgot: Mummy said to tell you white tie."

"For crying out loud! Who's coming?" His jaw dropped.

Flavia giggled.

"Darling, I can't ever remember these Embassy things—ambassadors and plenipotentiaries and potentates and—oh, do *you* remember when I was a kid and you or it may have been Mummy said something about a *chargé d'affaires*, and I thought it was Charger and I plastered myself to the window, expecting to see a glorious white horse in full—caparison, isn't it? And nothing came but a taxi, with a fat, rather common-looking little man in it?"

This was better, thought Ginever, as he joined in her laughter.

"And then," went on Flavia, between whoops, "I asked what had happened about the charger, and Mummy or perhaps it was you said he was it— Oh, Daddy!" She flung her arms round him and gazed up into his face, with parted lips and wide eyes that held, it seemed to George Ginever, all the glory and all the tragedy of her youth. "Wasn't it wonderful—being young, and not knowing anything about anything?"

And then Blythe walked in with a parcel which she handed to Flavia.

"Be an angel and take this down to Mrs. Roberts, she's waiting for it."

Chapter Eight

The weekend was over. He and Blythe were alone, virtually for the first time. They went into the dining room, and Ginever poured out pegs. Strangling a yawn, Blythe shook her head as he offered her the glass.

"No, thanks; it's too late." She repeated the yawn—he thought unconvincingly; but he realised he had come to suspect every gesture of Blythe's, no matter how innocent each might be, and that this was not the way to arrive at amicable conclusions. "What a god-awful play. Whoever thought it up deserves to be crucified.— Will you put the lights out?"

"Presently. Let's relax for a bit."

She capitulated with a faint shrug. The grimace that pulled down the corners of her mouth said without words, "All right; if this is it, let's get it over." She said across her shoulder, "You'd better fetch me that drink—and some cigarettes; I've smoked all mine."

"Have you got any plans?" she asked, when he joined her in the drawing room. So, thought Ginever, she had made up her mind, in those few minutes, to forestall him. He lit a pipe, taking his time over it; when he had felt her impatience tugging at him long enough, he dropped the match in a tray.

"Nothing very definite. And you?"

"After I've taken Flavia to school, I thought I'd stop out there for a while."

"Where? Lausanne?" Knowing her dislike for Switzerland, the inducement, he thought, must be powerful.

"Spain—perhaps," she said cautiously.

He was graciously pleased to observe that Spain, in February and March, sounded like a good idea. Málaga—all that strip of the coast, south to Gibraltar—was all right, apart from the Spring rains.

"I suppose," said Blythe, after a silence, "you've forgotten the lease runs out at the end of next year."

He admitted it had slipped his memory.

"So we'll have to start thinking about a move."

"So it's a good moment for reorganisation. As a matter of fact—I'm looking for a place to work in."

She raised her eyebrows and smiled at the tip of her cigarette, off which she tapped the ash.

"How odd."

"What's 'odd'? We've said for a long time the house was impossible."

"*You've* said. I like it," corrected Blythe. "But of course you need more space, and it's a good idea, to find somewhere else to work in. I don't know why you didn't think of it before."

He did not tell her that he had thought of it many times, and that it was only his fatal habit of procrastination, his dependence on other people for his decisions, that had made him put the idea aside.

"Look, my dear; let's come clean. We'd both like to remake our lives; isn't that it?" He waited and, as she remained silent, ploughed on. "Isn't it just a question of who divorces who?"

"Adultery or desertion; those are the standard grounds for divorce, aren't they?" She did not even trouble to look surprised. "I suppose I could have divorced you half a dozen times. But you didn't want it, did you?"

He could have retorted, "And neither did you!"

While he sought for words that were not likely to arouse the antagonism that seemed always to smoulder under the surface of their lightest exchanges, Blythe said with a fine smile:

"I'm afraid you'd find it very difficult to divorce me!"

"That's as may be. I'd certainly prefer it to go the other way."

She turned her head away quickly, and her face was hidden by the autumn-leaf fall of her hair. He remembered times when he must have hurt her deeply, and humiliated her, and left her feeling lost. He remembered moments—far past—when they had been, or seemed to be, everything to each other. He remembered, and felt brutal in remembering, that she had reached the age when some women have a sudden, desperate quickening, and hoped with all his heart that she would not for some reason of ancient grudges force the initiative upon him. An old childhood's saying came back to him: "Biting off your nose to spite your face!" Blythe would certainly be "biting off her nose" if she obliged him to divorce her. For goodness' sake, why could she not come clean, as he was prepared to do, and let them talk this out amicably—with due recognition of the important part Flavia must play in the disposition of their future.

"I suppose it's the Lucy girl."

"Luce. She was christened Lucian."

"Extraordinary name. Well—what's the difference between this and the others?"

Prepared as he was for this question, Ginever had not yet found the answer; that is to say, in his soul he knew it, but he had not had time to work out the verbal formula that Blythe (and doubtless others) would naturally expect. He reflected that he might have done better, from Blythe's point of view, to put this all down on paper, in the form of a letter, and wondered, not for the first time, why a writer was supposed,

117

by the nature of his trade, to be able to talk. Many could do so, spontaneously; only he knew the hundreds of hours that went into the preparation of his lectures, and the labour that went into the apparent spontaneity of his delivery. (Over that, also, Blythe had helped in early days.) His mind worked too slowly, he supposed, for the impromptu, and the privacy which exists between the writer and his sheet of paper was absolutely necessary for the clarification of his ideas.

"I can't tell you. It's different. That's all," he answered her question.

"Do you mean—you expect me to take you seriously, this time?"

The "this time" went just that little too far. She knew as well as he did that he had never previously suggested divorce. Their quarrels, which had grown more and more indifferent and languid with the passage of time, ended invariably with Blythe's declaration, "Well, I'm not going to divorce you; it would be too silly!"—and he had a guilty sense of relief, for, of course, in his innermost, he had not wanted to add to his responsibilities, and had been honest enough with himself— and, he hoped, with others it concerned—not to contemplate making a permanency out of an easy and elastic attachment.

He waited until his anger was under control, and spoke carefully.

"Let's look at it like this. We aren't, either of us, getting much out of the present arrangement. Why shouldn't we both have another chance?"

"Chance of what?"

"We aren't getting younger—"

"Thanks for the memory," she breathed, and George prayed inwardly to be preserved from losing his temper.

"But there's no reason there shouldn't be plenty of happiness ahead for both of us, if we have a bit of consideration for each other."

"Happiness," said Blythe, "is a strictly private matter."

He granted her that, and said there was no reason for her grudging that to him, or him to her.

"Who's grudging?" asked Blythe, with arched brows.

"You are, at the moment. I've come clean; why can't you?"

"What do you imagine I've got to come clean about?"

He could not but admire her bravado.

"I don't know; but I suppose the lawyers would sort that out."

"Are you threatening something?"

"I'm not threatening anything. I'm prepared to offer you all the evidence for a perfectly decent, not at all scandalous, divorce. If you don't choose to act on the evidence, I'll be obliged to take steps, and ask for 'discretion.' The one thing I'm not prepared to do is hang about indefinitely, waiting for you to make up your mind. Luce and I want to get married. Nothing's going to stop that, believe me."

"You don't expect me to make up my mind about a thing like this in five minutes."

"Five minutes nothing! It's ten years since marriage meant anything to either of us; you know that as well as I do. You've been generous, so we've gone on being friends. I'd like that to continue—"

"Why not?" she shrugged.

"Because, on present terms, it isn't possible. For either of us. Let's be honest. We've failed to make a 'go' of it, and it's my fault: absolutely and entirely. I've given you a rotten deal, and you've been wonderful. I'm offering you the easy way out—"

"And supposing I don't want to take it?"

"Well, I do," said George bluntly. "I'm going to marry Lucian van Thal. And if you won't divorce me— What is it? What's stopping you?" he burst out. "What's the idea of living the way we are—married and yet not married?"

"I haven't said I won't divorce you, but I'm not going to

119

be rushed into anything," said Blythe. "What's the rush, anyhow? Is Lucy going to have a baby, or something?"

Controlling himself, he said this had nothing to do with the situation, but that Luce was not, to his knowledge, pregnant.

"That's just as well. I don't care for having a pistol held to my head," said Blythe coolly. "And, of course, there's Flavia; she mightn't take to the idea."

At three in the morning—having laboured through a cloud of evasions, denials, half-admissions, and recantations, on Blythe's part, they had got no further. The only clear point was that she had not so far agreed to divorce him. And why? Heaven might know but not George Ginever. She had not even admitted to having a lover, and this led to the suspicion on Ginever's part, that she did not feel secure in her attachment; that she could not face a future without the moral support of a husband; that a semi-detached husband was better, to her, than none. In consideration of Blythe's character, of the disproportionate importance she lent to social values, this did not appear to be far from the truth. Blythe was a snob, and there is no more helpless creature on earth when its trappings of snobbery are removed! The snail dragged from its shell is, in comparison, armoured like the 'dillo'!

It was strange how, over the years of their marriage, their positions had reversed themselves. To begin with, Blythe was the leader—almost, it might be said, the *dompteuse* of a promising young husband who, as time went on, established himself and, without awareness on his part, took the lead: the very thing for which she had worked with passion and devotion, even before they were married. And, having achieved it, was apparently content to bask in reflected glory. Apparently; that was the operative word. Behind that bright and shining façade of Mrs. George Ginever lurked what painful uncertainties?

("Here's Mrs. Leo Hunter!" A shrill voice behind his shoulder in the foyer at a first night caught Ginever's ear; perhaps he was in one of his over-sensitive moods. As Blythe swam up, with the President of the Royal Academy and a fashionable architect in her train, he realised, with resentment on her behalf, that the speaker was referring to her; and in the next moment the pair of them were exchanging "Darlings!" Blythe was on her way to becoming one of those old harridans who, between the wars, ruled the waves of literary and artistic society, and were avoided by every honest writer or painter. But she had not got their copper-plated, iron-riveted assurance; there was something terribly and touchingly soft behind the act she put on. She would never make it, as old Sunya Vaughan, old Lettice Carfax, old "Topaze" Newark had made it. Anyhow, the times were against her. That night, at the Haymarket, was the first time the disparity in their ages was driven in on Ginever; he was shocked, angry, compassionate, and suddenly protective towards Blythe—whose brilliant make-up, elegant gown, and complete self-possession disclaimed protection. She introduced him to the woman, now linked arm-in-arm with her, who had described her as Mrs. Leo Hunter. As he politely accepted the introduction, he wondered if Blythe had any friends; any real friends.)

That he was determined, come hell or high water, to have his freedom, Blythe could not, or would not, grasp. She must, she said, discuss it with someone else before coming to any sort of decision—which was fair enough.

"Well, my dear, I've laid all my cards on the table. I wish you'd do the same."

"What cards?" Frequently using them herself, Blythe always professed contempt of verbal clichés.

"I don't want"—he forced himself to keep his temper—"in any way to force your confidence. If we're going to break it up, surely we can do it on a friendly basis? Whether or not you believe me, I do care about you; about your happiness—"

"Yes; if you were able to persuade yourself I was 'happy' it would furnish you with a beautiful let-out, wouldn't it?"

"But for some unknown reason you aren't inclined to give me that 'let-out'; why not? For crying out loud, why not? Can't we both, at this last, be generous?"

"You've made some very funny insinuations," she said.

"All right; I'll stop insinuating. There's somebody you care about, isn't there? But there's some obstacle. I'm part of the obstacle. Right. Why not get rid of me to start with?"

"You are so simple," sneered Blythe. "'Get rid of!' As if that solved anything."

He refused to be outfaced by her scorn.

"So far as I'm concerned, it solves it all. If you won't take the easy way out, I'll have to act, through my solicitors. Which might be uncomfortable for everybody—including Flavia. Why the hell," he exploded, "can't you give me a simple divorce and go and get married—"

She went on, "You must get this into your head. You can't possibly divorce me."

"So you say. But if you persist in these obstructive attitudes, I'll have a dam' good try!"

"You'll be sorry!"

He was sorry already; sorry for her confusion and her inability to give a straight answer to a straight question. The uneasy thought crossed his mind, could Blythe possibly have got herself into a tangle of which she had cause to be ashamed? Had she fallen, or perhaps been trapped, into some indiscretion that involved more than the plain fact of marital infidelity? Ruthless as he was determined to be on Luce's account, his natural kindness asserted itself in one last attempt to gain her confidence.

"All right; don't make me sorry. Can't you tell me, if you're in trouble of some sort? Won't you let me help you—if I can?"— The absurdity of the appeal was apparent to both of them. She gave a faint, wintry smile.

"Sweet of you—don't be silly," she murmured. "Of course I'm not 'in trouble'—what sort of trouble could I be in? I'm awfully tired," she cried, with a kind of youthful petulance. "I'm absolutely worn out with all the to-dos over Flavia—and now you drop this on me, in the middle of the night, when I can't even think clearly—"

Careful, spoke a voice in Ginever's ear; Blythe, when she sounded the note of pathos, was at her most devious, most dangerous.

"Why's it got to be different this time?" she cried, repeating herself. "What's the difference between this Lucy, and all the others? You've got it badly this time: all right. Go off and live with her for a year—a couple of years—if you want to. By that time you'll know—and I'll know—if it's likely to last; and that will be time enough to talk about divorce."

"You know," said Ginever, "I could understand this, if we cared the least little bit about each other."

"Perhaps we do care"—on a whisper.

"That's enough of that." Her falsity disposed of the last bit of his regard for her; one can be kind, and generous, and care nothing. "Let's get this straight. I'm quitting. I'm not living here, under your roof, any longer."

"No, of course; you're going to set up house with Lucy."

"What I'm going to do with Lucy, as you call her, is no affair of yours. But I want to know, before you go away, what you propose to do about it. If you won't take action, I shall."

"The man of action!" She smiled thinly.

"Yes, I've earned that.— You've asked, What's the difference. Well, so far as I can sum it up, this time it's not only a matter of emotions. It's me—myself. I can't go on being a puppet."

"Do you know," said Blythe, after a long silence, "I think this Lucy has had a very unfortunate effect on you."

"It's nothing to do with Luce!"

"All right, darling, don't shout. But I don't understand this puppet-talk. Could you put it into words of one syllable, for my inferior intellect?"

"You know, if you say things like that, we'll quarrel. For God's sake, after all these years, do we have to quarrel?—All I've achieved—most that I've achieved," he corrected himself, "up to the present, has come to me through you."

"Nonsense. George, what maggot have you got in your brain? You've got a position of immense authority—"

"Oh God. Oh please." He clutched his head. "You and Harry Lasker, between you, have built up a piece of efficient machinery. A push-button miracle. Is there anything—anything real—behind that? Can't you see I've got to find out, before it's too late? Is there anything there—beyond the slick stuff that brings in the lolly and gets headlines and involves me with people I don't give a dam' for, and wouldn't give a dam' for me if I dropped out of the columns—?" He drew a deep breath. "We know everybody—everybody, don't we? So how many friends have we got?— I mean real friends, with no axes to grind—"

"I think you're being a bit hysterical," she said coolly. "And you're not being very fair, to me or Harry Lasker. You wanted independence, so—between us—we tried to give you what you wanted. It's not very gracious, now, to turn round and say—"

"At the moment," said Ginever, "I'm not concerned with graciousness. Not even with common politeness. Let's cut the smooth talk. I'm no good to you in bed, am I? You don't want me—and I don't want you. That's putting it crudely."

"So that's marriage," said Blythe, after a pause. "Going to bed. How very—Victorian!"

"You know as well as I do, marriage isn't just going to bed. If it were, our marriage wouldn't have lasted all these years."

"There was Martha Vining, Alice Reid, Pam Squire." She counted them off on her fingers; she used up the fingers of one hand and started on the other. "You went to bed with all of them—"

"Which shows how unimportant it is—going to bed. They didn't mean anything—and I didn't mean anything to them —and you know it. So you didn't waste time and trouble."

"No. I'm not silly—that way."

"You'd have been 'silly'—if you'd had a reason."

"I don't know what you mean"—loftily.

"If there'd been somebody you wanted to go to bed with."

"All this about 'bed'!"

"All right!" His temper, like the mirror, cracked from side to side. "Somebody—in or out of bed—you wanted to—"

"George!" Her face was suddenly invaded with dark, unbecoming colour. "Don't use that word in front of me! Keep it for your tarts."

A gale of inner rage swept him upwards; he seemed to hang in air—and then suddenly to drop. The whole thing had become unspeakably small and foolish, not worth while losing temper over. What was it—"all-embracing patience"? He could not rise to those heights! But he could keep his temper and keep his head and, by doing so, perhaps even force some approximation to truth out of this devious woman.

"Well, you've got somebody at last—"

"Who says so?"

"I say so. Do you think I'm so bloody dim as not to see—? It's infernally stupid of you, to set up this resistance; it only makes it harder for everybody—including yourself. Well—I suppose I can only let Cohen loose on it."

"Your tame Jew-boy!" she jeered; but something told him that behind her defiant façade she was scared. She had reason to be. The firm of Jewish lawyers to whom, on Harry Lasker's advice, he had transferred his literary business, with which the old-fashioned solicitors who had formerly handled his affairs and Blythe's were not qualified to cope, was likely, on their client's behalf, to be pretty ruthless. Well—she had brought it on herself.

"Flavia's got to be considered.— For God's sake, can't you

see," he exploded, "that the less fuss we make over this business, the better it is for Fla?"

"If you imagine I'm going to hand Fla over to you and Lucy—" she said, tight-lipped.

"There's no point in speaking as if Fla were a parcel, to be 'handed over' for your convenience or mine. She's got a will and a mind of her own. She's got a right to be in on this discussion, which affects her future as much as ours. It's going to help her, if she's in our confidence, and feels we're as much concerned with her affairs as with our own. And feels we're parting as friends, not as enemies."

"We're already enemies, Fla and I," said Blythe bitterly. "Go on: say it. Say it's my fault if we are!" she defied him.

"I'm not concerned with 'faults,' for the present. Isn't the first thing to make it as easy as possible for Fla? An undefended case doesn't make headlines—even in the rags, even if the name's Ginever!"

"Lovely and easy," she crooned. "You've always had it easy, haven't you? Everything's got to be easy.— Oh, for God's sake, let's go to bed."

She went round the room, mechanically putting out lights, beating up cushions, pushing chairs into their familiar design. They went out on the landing, and as Blythe pressed the switch down a shaft of light came up from the basement.

"Oh—the little beasts. They've done it again."

"Who've done what?"

"Fla's gang: they've been down in the kitchen."

"All right. I'll cope. Go to bed—and have a good night."

The kitchen, blazing with fluorescent, stank of burnt food. A burnt-out frying pan stood on the top of a red-hot ring. The table was littered with dirty mugs, cigarette butts, empty bottles of Coke. Broken plates were shulled under the sink, which was a mess of eggshells, burnt toast, and an abandoned can of ravioli. Wet towels, with scorch-marks, were

126

slopped on the floor. There was a girl's shabby handbag with, by the look of it, nothing inside it except perhaps a lipstick; a dirty glove; and a rag that might be a scarf. None of it went with the immaculate setting of Blythe's kitchen. She would have found it disgusting—he was glad he had come down alone. He found it sad.

He turned off the stove and opened the door into the area, to let in some fresh air. What appeared to be a bundle of clothing was stuffed in between the steps and the coal bunker. Ginever switched on the area light, and a tallowy face with red-rimmed eyes pulled itself out of the bundle.

"Come on; out." He gave the bundle a gentle push with his foot.

"Hi, man." The voice was indistinct and very young, by the sound, a youth of sixteen or seventeen. Ginever hoisted him to his feet; his breath smelt awful and hung in a cloud on the perishing air. Ginever pulled him into the warmth of the kitchen, pushed him into a chair, and he slithered off it on to the floor. He was suddenly and preposterously sick. Ginever left him being sick and found some coffee in a Cona, ready for the morning, transferred it to a pan, hotted it up, and gave it to him, black. He lay there on the floor, bent over his arms, with his head down, shuddering.

Ginever went upstairs. Flavia was lying on her back, gently snoring. He picked his way through the litter of clothes, food, and empty bottles, to shake her several times before she opened her eyes with the half-blind gaze of a nine-days kitten.

"Come on; get up."

"Whaffor? Whaddyou want?" She groaned and turned her face into the pillow. She did not resist as he pulled the dressing gown round her shoulders, found her slippers, and teased her bare toes into them. "Wha's—wha's 'a' matter?" as he made her stand up, and pushed her gently towards the stairs.

"Perhaps you'll be able to explain that," said Ginever.

Now wide awake, she gave him a look of alarm.

The youth had got so far as to prop himself against the legs of a chair; the coffee, untouched, was by his side. He gave Flavia a sickly grin and said "Hi."

"Hi," said Flavia, sounding stunned. Then she caught sight of the pool of vomit and jerked her head away, with an expression of disgust and shame. Ginever felt sorry for her. He lit a cigarette and sat down on the corner of the table.

"Well—who's your friend?"

"I don't know. Were—were you at my party?" she stammered. She was pathetically taken aback.

Apparently incapable of anything but a sickly grin, the youth managed to hoist himself to his feet—kicking over the cup of coffee—and started to weave towards the door.

"Hold it," said Ginever.

The kid hitched a shoulder towards his ear and stood sullen.

"I done nothin', daddy-O!" His speech was a mixture of cockney and movie-tone American: the current idiom of the gangs. He sounded at once defiant and scared. Neither he nor Ginever was prepared for Flavia's reaction.

"And don't say daddy-O to my father!— I'm sorry. I don't know what he's doing here; I expect he came with somebody."

"'He came with somebody!'" the youth mocked her. "Don't give us that blow, chick!"

"Clear out," said Ginever distinctly. The youth stank of bad breath, hair oil, and something more, that made him ruthless. "Clear out, before I get the cops on you."

"What on earth's going on down there?"— Blythe's voice floated down the stairwell.

Flavia shot him an anguished look.

"For God's sake, don't let her come down!"

"Fla; do you know what time it is?"

"Yes, I'm just putting the lights out. Go on, go on; I can manage this," she hissed, pushing him towards the door.

"George!" said Blythe's imperative voice, and the heels of her mules clacked on the stairs.

"Daddy!"

The boy had slid out.

Ginever caught Blythe halfway down the stairs and managed to manoeuvre her back to her bedroom, where she stood in front of the glass, angrily brushing out her pretty hair, and he gave her a version—bowdlerized less for Flavia's sake than for her own—of the situation.

"Absolutely outrageous!" stormed Blythe. "All I can say is, roll on, Lausanne!"

He went up to Flavia's room and sat down on the bed. Shortly afterwards, an exhausted figure staggered in.

"I've locked up and put the lights out. I've cleaned up the mess—" she shuddered.

"So we oughtn't to have gone down in the kitchen." She had dropped into a chair. "Fair enough; Mummy gave me this room to have my friends—and do more or less as we please. Sandra and Chess hadn't had a square meal since yesterday, and Sandra's pregnant. I'd only got Coke and beer and crisps and fancy bits up here. You don't grudge a few eggs and some stuff out of the freezer to a pregnant girl!"

"No. But you can't claim pregnancy for the character I collected off the garbage bins."

"You oughtn't to have threatened him with the cops, Daddy!— Of course, you didn't mean it," said Flavia.

"Would it surprise you that I did mean it?"

"You can't do that to my friends."

"Friends? You use the word too lightly. You didn't even know his name. Or did you? Be honest."

"We don't bother about names," she said distantly. "And you can't talk about police to my friends."

"I'm afraid, in the circumstances, I can."

"What do you mean?"

"I suppose you know what's a reefer," said Ginever.

"Reefer? Well, really, Daddy!" With a curl of the lip, she scorned the imputation of ignorance. But as the implication of his question penetrated her, her defence broke down. "But you don't—you don't suppose—?"

"I don't know what I suppose; I don't want to suppose anything. I don't want to interfere with your friendships—your real friendships. This is your mother's house. Do you think it's fair to have people here who might involve her—and all of us—in a lot of unpleasantness?"

"But I don't know what you're getting at."

"I think you do. You seem to be having people here who wouldn't be acceptable to her—or, if it comes to that, to me."

"Oh—'class'!" she sneered.

"'Class' be damned; the word's obsolete. If there's any 'class,' it means people who have the same standards of behaviour: of honourable behaviour, and decency."

"We've got our own 'honour' and 'decency.' We happen to think it's as good as yours," said Flavia loftily. "Mummy thinks we spend our time gaping at TV, playing the pops, doing the twist. Of course we do all that: we like Adam Faith and all that. That's all surface. We've got to take time off."

"Time off from what?" he persisted.

"From the things that matter."

He asked her what, in her opinion, mattered, and she gave him a look out of the corner of her eye, obviously making up her mind whether he was to be trusted.

"Well, for one thing," she muttered, "'If you would fall into any extreme, let it be on the side of gentleness.'"

"That's good enough." He was deeply touched. "Who said it?"

"St. Francis de Sales; as a matter of fact, I got it off a calendar," she admitted, and pointed to the leaf pinned up over her bed. "I think it's pretty good. Anyhow, it's constructive; it isn't a 'you mustn't' or 'you can't.'"

"The principle is grand; its application—couldn't that depend on circumstances? Gentleness can be as out of place as brutality."

"It's safer; on people like me, it's obligatory. I've had all the advantages, all the privileges."

He asked, presently, if she had ever smoked a reefer.

"Once—just a bit—for fun. But what's all this reefer business?"

"Are reefers smoked up here, at your parties?"

"Daddy, you're crackers. What do you take us for?"

"That doesn't answer my question, but I won't press it. I'm just giving you warning. If that character, or anybody like him, comes into the house again, by or without your invitation, I'll take steps. For their own protection. And yours."

"I don't see why," said Flavia, after a pause, "we've got to be treated like juvenile delinquents because our views are at odds with those of people like you. We try to be honest to ourselves. We're not a lot of lay-abouts, as Mummy seems to think; we don't smoke hemp. If that kid—I haven't a clue about him: never saw him before tonight—smokes hemp, he's probably a show-off; he's got a misery behind him that obliges him to do anything that's against the law. Well, that doesn't put him outside, does it? We're lucky—most of us. So there's room for him—if he wants it. But mostly they don't want it.

"We aren't good-timers, as everybody seems to think. I don't mean there aren't some good-timers," she allowed. "They're silly twerps, and nice, and lots of fun. But they don't belong."

"Belong to what?"

"To the Group," she mumbled. She gave him a look of profound distrust.

"Well—you know all about this Ban the Bomb business: marching and sitting down and all the jazz."

Yes, said Ginever, he had read the papers.

"Some of them do it for fun. They come up in the juvenile courts, and nobody takes them seriously, and it does more

131

harm than good. Most of them are my age, or younger. But they could help, if they were organised. I sat down one Saturday," admitted Flavia, "and I was mad I didn't get picked up. So we worked out a sort of plan. I don't suppose you're interested—"

"Go on," said Ginever.

"Well, the best way we can help—I mean, my age group—is to build up a fund to pay off fines. Baby-sitting, helping at coffee bars, do-it-yourself jobs. We pay in as much as we can afford into the fund."

"Is it working out?"

"Fairly well. Some of the kids cheat and some won't play, because of course there's a lot more fun to be had out of the sit-downs and getting their names in the papers. But we're converting them. I think we are," said Flavia seriously. "We've paid off a lot of fines. Some of them think it's more impressive to go to prison, but it isn't, really. It's waste of man-power. We've paid six fines, and costs, for one girl alone; she's an out-of-work actress and she hasn't got a bean, but she's terrific! A sort of Joan of Arc. She's one of our best speakers.

"Mummy calls us a lot of little half-baked Communists. We do have some Communists, and that's a pity; it creates prejudice among people—I mean important, influential people—who might back us up. But, Daddy: what's politics got to do with wanting to survive?—or with trying to save human beings from another Hiroshima? The politicians and scientists are forcing racial suicide on us: we don't *want* to commit racial suicide!

"You know, they're mad," she went on incoherently. "Pouring millions into the exploration of space, and at the same time millions into the destruction of Earth. I can't go to Lausanne," she cried, "while there are all these terrible things to think about, and struggle against. Lausanne—Switzerland —the plushy hide-out for everybody who wants to evade his responsibilities to his country, his government, the ordinary commitments of an ordinary human being to his own little world—society—whatever you like to call it—"

He silently cursed the state of the world which had made a child of Flavia's age aware of her "responsibilities."

"Let's go on with this after we've had some sleep. Let's take a day off; go down to Brighton and have one of our fuddles round the Lanes," he suggested.

"Smashing!" She brightened, then flushed and bit her lip. "Oh, blast; I don't believe I can."

"So what's the cock and bull this time?"

"It's not cock and bull! I just happen to have promised— you don't have to look as if I'm lying!" she burst out. "If you want to know, it's Sandra; she's got to go to the clinic at lunch-time, and I said I'd take over for her in the shop. Somebody's got to; it's the only time in the day they do any trade, and what with her baby coming, and everything, they simply can't afford to lose sales. Don't you *see*, Daddy? When you've given your word, you don't—" She was rattling on, when he interrupted.

"Just a minute, will you? I suppose you realise I've not had more than ten minutes of your company since I came home?"

"Of course I do," muttered Flavia. "I'm sorry. It's just one of those things."

"All right, but I've had enough of 'those things.' I've got a pretty full schedule for the next fortnight, but I can clear tomorrow—I mean today. I'll be waiting for you at half past eleven; that will give you time to come to some other arrangement with your friend."

"But I've told you—" She bit her lip. "I can't arrange anything—they're not even on the telephone—"

"A shop—not on the telephone?"

"It's only a little lock-up—down the Kensington Road," stammered Flavia. "They sell second-hand stuff—books—or anything they happen to pick up—"

"That'll do, Fla. We'll drop round by there and you can do your explaining." He was determined this time to put a stop to her evasions.

"It just happens," she told him icily, "that this isn't the sort of thing that can be fixed with 'explanations.' Chess and Sandra don't keep their shop for fun! And some mornings they don't take a penny—and if it weren't for lunch-time, it wouldn't be worth opening. If it comes to that, the shop doesn't even belong to them; it belongs to a dotty old uncle of Chess's—but when Sandra started the baby, and they got married—"

"It doesn't sound very profitable," said Ginever, trying to sound sympathetic.

"They don't care much about money, but of course they've got to sleep somewhere, and feed."

The solution seemed, to Ginever, pretty simple. He was willing, if necessary, to buy his daughter's company. Changing the subject, he observed:

"We've got a lot of things to talk about, and not a lot of time before you go away."

"So I *am* going to Lausanne," she breathed, after a silence.

"Unless you can think up some excellent reason against. You made us promise not to send you to English boarding school."

"Yes, I did."

"And, last year, you were all for 'going abroad.'"

"Yes, I was. You get these notions, when you're young. I've grown a different set of values, since then."

"You don't have to abandon your values, do you, at Lausanne?"

She shrugged her shoulders disdainfully; the question was not worth answering.

"You failed your G.C.E. That was a pity, wasn't it? You didn't have to."

"It was just a bore, Daddy. There were so many more important things."

"That's silly, Fla. You know as well as I do that education's important."

"Education?" She gave a shrill, unbelieving laugh. "Do you imagine I'm being sent to Lausanne for the sake of education? It's high time you came home, Daddy!" she shouted, ending confusedly, "though what you're going to do about it goodness knows. There's one thing you've got to understand: I'm no longer the dear little blue-eyed innocent! My eyes are big and green"—she widened them at him—"and they see things I don't like. And I don't even understand—properly. And that's why I'm being sent to Lausanne!"

While he sat, shocked into silence, she flung her arms wildly round his neck.

"Promise me something! That, whatever happens, you and me'll be together—always."

The thin, winter dawn was already in the sky when Ginever regained his bedroom. Could he ever forgive Blythe? he wondered, at the same time wondering about the oddly puritan approach of the younger generation to a situation which was —regrettably—commonplace. Evidently Flavia knew something that her mother might, in decency, have kept from her. And, if she took Blythe's infidelity so hard, what was she going to say to him and Luce?

Flavia was waiting for him at half past eleven; white-of-egg pale, with purple rings under her eyes, he was wrung with pity for the tired child, who had had, at most, three or four hours of sleep. The fur collar of a pale overcoat clasped her delicate chin, her pony-tail was rolled up in a tight coil on the top of her small head, and her thin, adolescent legs ended in little sealskin boots. She could have been fifteen, or twenty-five, or even thirty-five—according to contemporary style.

135

She was strangulated with self-consciousness; she hardly uttered, during the tedious threading of traffic.

A grey-faced child in a dirty smock looked up as they entered the shop. There were some shelves littered with tattered paper-backs and a couple of boxes filled with the rejects of pre-war novels. A sagging string carried hangers with murky clothing and a table some deplorable bits of glass, china, and metal. Flavia muttered, "Here's Father," and need not, he felt, have sounded so ashamed. The girl got up clumsily, displaying the signs of her pregnancy. While she and Flavia mumbled, Ginever examined the stock; there was nothing he could honestly buy. He made a little collection of the less grimy novels, and added to it a piece of badly chipped glass, possibly Bristol.

"What do you want that muck for?" brusquely demanded the girl. He was so taken aback that, for a moment, he was unable to formulate a reply; he laughed foolishly. He put down a pound note, and she looked at it, and at him, as though he were crazy. "I can't change that," she snapped. "Sixpence—ninepence"—she scuffed through the books. "Five and four for the lot, counting the glass. But you don't want it!" she accused him again. Her face was crimson, and so was Flavia's. As he fished the coins out of his pocket, five shillings and fourpence did not seem much to pay for the pleasure of his daughter's company.

Flavia did not utter until they were on the outskirts of Croydon. They were held up by traffic lights when she burst out:

"You mustn't ever do that sort of thing again!"

"What sort of thing?"

"That beastly, patronising act you pulled on Sandra."

"Oh, shut up! I wasn't patronising."

The expedition was not, from Ginever's point of view, a success. Flavia was polite, superficially interested as they wandered through the Lanes, which, as a child, she had loved. She had apparently lost her interest in collecting; showed no enthusiasm for a particularly beautiful old "snow-storm" paperweight he offered her (the sort of thing she would have been "crazy" about, a few years before), and hung about, in evident boredom, while he priced some crystal which matched up with the two big honey jars he had given Luce as one of her Christmas presents.

When Flavia was little, this had been one of their favourite outings; the antique shops, to her, were super toy shops. She had genuinely loved the oddments they picked up. Knowing nothing of values, she loved equally something costing a few pence or as many pounds. Blythe was inclined to mock, not unkindly, at their antiquarian ramblings, which Ginever claimed were helping to educate the child's taste. "Don't be silly! A kid of that age doesn't have taste." "You're probably right; but there's something in the historic sense, it means something, to handle a toy, or a cup, made for a kid of Fla's age, who's been dead a hundred years. It doesn't matter if it's ugly or beautiful; it's a link in the chain. It's awareness of what went before . . ."

He had foolishly counted on this evocation of the past to help break down the tension between them. He was aware, when they sat down to an elaborate luncheon, that his little plan had failed. Flavia had relaxed, to the extent of being chatty and friendly—as she might have been to any casual acquaintance. But at any mention of Blythe she froze into silence.

Taking the bull by the horns, he brought up, once again, the subject of Lausanne.

"Look, if you don't want Lausanne, what would you rather?"

She lowered her eyes, lifted her fine brows towards the neat, up-drawn line of her hair.

"There's no point in discussing it, is there?— Since

my mother"—Ginever started; Blythe had always been "Mummy," never "my mother"—"since my mother," she repeated, "and Oggie Schneider have got it all tied up, the way they want it."

. . . This isn't true, thought George Ginever. It positively isn't true.

Chapter Nine

When he came out of the barber's, a little, fat, businessman was paying off his taxi, and Ginever lifted his umbrella to signal to the driver—then, as it dawned on him that the businessman had exquisite ankles and stiletto heels, he remembered that he and Olga Schneider had patronised the same hairdresser for a number of years. Their cuts were, in fact, practically identical; longish on top, short back and sides, left-side parting. She was groping in the pockets of her short, tight skirt; Oggie never carried a handbag, but kept her change loose, like a man. Failing to find what she wanted, she plunged her hand inside the mink lining of her tweed overcoat and produced a wallet, from which she scowlingly extracted a pound note. At this moment she caught sight of Ginever.

"Hi; have you got half a crown about you?"

"I can change a pound, madam," the man was saying. Ignoring him, she stuffed the note back in her wallet, accepted Ginever's half-crown, added it to the one in her hand, and passed the two coins to the driver, who looked at them speechlessly, glanced at his clock (which said four and ninepence), and asked if she was sure she could afford it. It takes a millionairess, thought Ginever amusedly, to give a London taxi-driver a threepenny tip.

Pulling her glove on over her big diamond rings, Oggie smiled up at him; she had a delightful smile, which pursed her lips and drew her eyes into little crescents between the fine line of her brows and her plump cheekbones. Although he had every reason for not being pleased with Oggie, that smile of hers was irresistible: it recalled one of their minor tiffs.

"Stinking habit of yours, George, of putting your friends into your books."

"Most of 'em take it as a compliment. Come off it, Oggs" —guessing to what she referred, he grinned broadly. "You're not averse to a bit of publicity yourself!"

"Ha—that description of my 'cosily dissipated smile' lost me a job on which I was counting," she pouted.

He roared with laughter, in which, eventually, she joined.

"You are a bastard!"

"And you're another. What do you want with 'jobs'?" he mocked her.

"What do you think I do—sit round on my fanny swigging Scotch on the rocks and phoning my stockbroker?"

"No; now and again you buy villas in Ischia or Andalucian ranches! What happened to that *Schloss* you bought up?" he teased her. Taking it with her usual good humour, she swore at him; Oggie had the ripest vocabulary of profanity he had come across, he saluted it with respect. There was a night after one of her parties—when Oggie read Beddoes to the three or four survivors, among whom were himself and Blythe, in her voice of a poet *manqué*. They were all high—Oggie herself probably the highest of the lot. In her cups she had a kind of majesty; she was Queen Victoria—plus. Virginia was crumpled in a corner of the hearth, by the dead fire, her head sunk in her hands. And Blythe, her eyes half-closed, her face drained with fatigue, sat on the floor, on the tigerskin, and propped her head on her arm.

"Come, lift your head from that sad pillow, lady.
Let comfort kiss thee dry."

"Hate changin' notes and weighin' my pockets down with a
lot of filthy coppers. Nice to see you back, George; you look as
if New York agrees with you."

Ginever slipped the taxi-man a shilling, and nodded to him
to drive off.

"What d'you do that for?— They're all stinkin' with
money. Where are you goin'? Come in a minute."

She stepped smartly, with her gait of a miniature Guards-
man, past the commissionaire, who swung the door wide open
and tore off a smashing RAF salute. Ginever burst out laughing, and she cocked a suspicious eye at him.

"What's the big laugh?"

"I've been coming here a ripe ten years, but so far I don't
rate a salute from Pepper!"

"Try a Christmas box," said Oggie dryly. "Look: I'm not
havin' a 'do' this mornin'; I just want to pick up a parcel, then
we'll nip into the local for a quick one."

Oggie's local being the Ritz and her notion of a quick one
an hour's session, Ginever glanced at his watch. He had two
appointments, one with his accountants in Vigo Street, the
other with Harry Lasker, and was supposed to lunch at the
Caprice with Bill Littlejohn, who might—or might not—bring
his play into London. But this chance encounter with Oggie
brought to a head all the mental confusion which had cheated
him of sleep since his conversation with Flavia. Whatever inconvenience it involved, he must not let the opportunity
pass; he would never get the truth from Blythe, but he might
get it from Oggie. Their relationship had always been more
than friendly, practically confidential. She had known about
his affairs, and he about hers—within formal limits, within a
pattern of allusions. She was gentlemanly, and so—he hoped—
was he. He liked and respected Oggie and believed the feeling

141

to be reciprocal. Her sexual pattern differed from the normal; whose business was that? Exclusively Oggie's.

He relieved her of a parcel. When they came out it had started to snow, and it took nearly ten minutes to get a taxi. He enquired what Oggie was doing, tooling around in taxis.

"Serves me bloody right; I got a new chauffeur and the perisher took me out yesterday and got us into every possible balls up between Piccadilly and Richmond, so I sacked him this morning.— Let's go back to the flat," she said, as at last the commissionaire signalled from the door. "I hate these buggering taxis!—and I don't walk"—it was two minutes from the Ritz to the flat.

There was the usual manservant on the door and foreign maids flickered in the background.

"We'll go in the drawing room. The music room's being redecorated"—among her many gifts, Oggie, he remembered, was no mean musician, and a considerable patron of the opera in London, Milan, and New York—"and I've got a girl doing some typing in the study. Go in and get warm while I take my things off."

"May I use your telephone?"

She nodded, and nodded to the man who moved forward, took his coat, and opened a door.

"Can I get your number for you, sir?"

He shook his head and took the receiver, dialled the Vigo Street number, and said he would be late. Then he rang the Lasker offices and said he probably wouldn't be able to make it. Harry sounded petulant. He was going up to Edinburgh; a film contract had come up and needed discussion.

"Discuss it with yourself, old boy," said Ginever, and gently put the receiver back on its cradle.

He and Blythe had often been to Oggie's parties, but he had never before seen the room by daylight. It was impressive, with its tall windows overlooking the Green Park and, distantly, the Palace, now obliterated in a flurry of snow. The heat, as usual, was tropical, for which the wood fire burning in the big Adam grate was not responsible. His eye caught the elaborately gilded mouldings of the ceiling, which he recognised, for the first time, as *trompe l'oeil*; he had seen the same sort of thing in Florence. It must be fun, to be able to indulge in that sort of extravagance.

Virginia's portrait had disappeared from over the fireplace and was replaced by rather a mediocre Dutch still life. Artistically speaking, this was an improvement; the portrait—*oeuvre* of one of Oggie's protégées—was not up to its surroundings; Virginia, who had taste, had always disliked it, but it pleased Oggie, who was easily led astray down the dubious corridors of contemporary art. Staring at the glass, the grapes, the dead feathers which had replaced the pearls and pale shoulders, he wondered how soon another portrait would hang there.

They had certainly made a clean sweep. Virginia's tapestry screen had gone, and her needlework cabinet from which, while Mozart or Bartók sounded through the archway that led to the music room, she produced her petit point, or the collages in bits of felt and fur and beads she sometimes exhibited in a gallery partly subsidised by Oggie in a mews off Mount Street. The innocent feminine litter she scattered about any room she happened to occupy had vanished. An impersonal tidiness suggested that, since Virginia's departure, Oggie had given up the use of the drawing room, and retreated, perhaps, into her study. For all the heat, there was a kind of death-chamber chill.

He hoped she would not beat about the bush. Would let them get it over as quickly and decently as possible.

The butler came in with champagne, followed by Oggie, who had changed into black velvet slacks; her plump chin was supported by a black satin stock. Mourning for the dear departed? Oggie favoured spectacular checks and lively chromes for indoor wear. He found himself instinctively bowing his head—and shaking it at the same time at the offer of one of her thin, dark cheroots. He spun the wheel of his lighter, and she shook her head at that, preferring a match.

"So where'm I going to get a chauffeur?"—this for the benefit of the butler, topping the glasses with Oggie's invariable pre-luncheon drink of champagne.

"So where'm I going to find a studio?" Ginever riposted. Her bright little eyes flickered; she took a pull on her weed.

"Pulling out, are you?" You had to admire Oggie's nerve!

"I want some more space for my work. I suppose you know our lease is up next year. But I've got to find something temporary."

"Temporary meaning—?" She dismissed the man with a nod.

"Until we've settled the future."

Oggie pulled a clean, man-sized handkerchief out of the pocket of her slacks, flapped it open, blew her nose, and tapped the ash off her cheroot with the tip of a scrupulously manicured little finger, circled with a big signet ring. The lump of cornelian and its intaglio, heavily set in Victorian gold, were familiar. Soon after their marriage, Blythe had offered it to him, but it was too small. "You could have it enlarged. It was Grandpa's; he was a very thin old man." "I don't like altering authentic pieces." "It's no good to me," shrugged Blythe, dropping it back in her jewel case.

"So she's told you."

"She hasn't told me anything."

"The little creep," said Oggie—but fondly. "I guessed she wouldn't. Well—that's how it is. So where do we go from here?"

She had a kind of gentlemanly off-handedness and appeared to have no curiosity about how Ginever came by his information.

"I want a divorce," he said bluntly.

"Fair enough," said Oggie.

"Nothing to do with this." He managed to keep his voice impersonal. "I told her I'll provide all the evidence."

She nodded, puffed out a cloud of smoke, and gazed through it at the *trompe l'oeil* of the cornice before replying.

"So we sit around while she makes up her mind. If she ever does," said Oggie dryly. "Cross fingers; heads you win, tails I lose!"

"What's winning? What's losing?— I want—"

"My dear George!" She gave him her charming smile. "It's not what you want, or what I want! It never has been—so far as Blythe's concerned. It's what she wants—and the bother of it is, she can't make up her mind.

"She's always had her cake and eaten it; you know that, better than I. So she wants to go on the way she's always gone on. To be Mrs. George Ginever means a lot to her. To come straight out and set up house with me means a break she can't face—for the present. Vee and I kept house, nine years. That blew up—as you probably know—while you were in the States; after I came out with Blythe, when you were in hospital. Vee got jealous, and there was the usual razmataz, and she went off to Antibes with Beryl Alton, and"—she ended with a shrug—"I don't much care for living by myself."

"Look, Oggie; it's no business of mine, if you and Blythe are in love. All I want's to get married."

"Sure." She lit another cheroot. "We've got to find a pretty powerful inducement, to make Blythe let go of you. If it were a man, she'd divorce at the drop of a hat; she'd go off and get married again—that would be fine. But she's ashamed of being in love with a woman. Until she's got over that, she's no good to me. Fair enough?"

He agreed it was fair enough.

"I don't want to pry into your affairs, Oggie—but I suppose you're joining Blythe after the trip to Lausanne?"

"She told you that, did she?"

"She told me that after she had taken Flavia to school she

was staying out there for a while—I think she said something about Málaga. Blythe isn't good at holidaying by herself—as no doubt you know. If she'd been joining up with the Locks or the Heslops she'd have mentioned it."

"Uh-huh. Well," said Oggie, after a pause. Her small, firm lips pursed themselves round the butt of her cheroot. As Ginever was starting to speak she silenced him with an imperious gesture. "Wait. Hold it. Now, supposing I don't go to Málaga?"

"That's up to you," he shrugged. "I don't see what difference it's going to make, either way."

"Don't you? Look," said Oggie, with the patience one shows to a backward child. "The present position is unsatisfactory for all three of us, isn't it? Right?"

"Right," nodded Ginever.

"And the only person who can resolve it is Blythe. And you'll agree with me it's about as easy to get a grip on Blythe as it is to hold a greased viper. I don't mean that unpleasantly; I happen," grinned Oggie, "to have a taste for snakes. I might tell you about that someday: it's quite a story. But we aren't sitting here to swop life-histories.

"If I don't turn up at the what's-it hotel, it just might dawn on her that I'm not standing for any more nonsense, see?"

"You mean, let her go out there to meet you, and then—?" He was shocked to realise he had not, in him, this element of ruthlessness. Oggie's bright eyes were fixed on him derisively.

"I've got as big a stake in this as you have. She's got to be driven into a decision. I'm prepared to administer shock tactics. If you've got any suggestions—" She invited him to produce them with a wave of the hand.

He admitted that the situation had dropped on him out of the blue, and that he had had no time to adjust to it. If Blythe persisted in her aversion from divorcing him, he had made it plain he would divorce her. That was simple enough, allowed Oggie, so long as Blythe would play ball. A smart firm of lawyers would deal with that—but they would naturally want co-operation.

"I don't think you'd find it easy to prove desertion—which would give you a respectable get-out—if she chooses to dig her toes in. Why don't you get an American divorce?"

"Because it wouldn't be legal over here, and I don't want to cut myself off, on account of Fla.— And, in regard to Fla"—a little flame of anger beat up in him—"you don't, either of you, seem to have shown much consideration for her."

"In what way?"

"She's not a fool. Why on earth couldn't you keep your affairs to yourselves?"

She gave him a sudden straight look.

"I had no idea that Flavia knew anything at all about it. Bloody clumsy of Blythe." Her indignation was genuine. You couldn't help liking Oggie: even believing in her—up to a point.

"Look: there's no point in our quarrelling, you and me. We haven't even the motive of jealousy. You don't care what, so long as you can get rid of Blythe. I don't care what, so long as she can get rid of you. She means nothing to you and you mean nothing to her. I've got a stinking reputation, and so, if I may say so," grinned Oggie, "have you. I've heard plenty about you, and I don't doubt you've heard plenty about me. There's one thing, according to the record, of which we're not guilty—either of us. We've never broken up happy homes.

"Having one object in view, we ought to be able to help each other. I've got no enmity towards you, and you shouldn't have any towards me. If I've got a bit more influence, at the moment, than you—which isn't saying much—we might use it to our mutual advantage."

"There's only one thing matters to me: that's Fla. I'm going to get custody—if it means sending the balloon up."

"Think that over," advised Oggie. The butler was at her elbow.

147

"The cook would like to know, how many for luncheon, madam."

"Have a chop, George," she invited.

"Thanks, Oggie; I've got a date."

"The usual," she told the man, and coolly dismissed the subject of their former conversation. "I might be able to help you over that studio business. What do you want?"

He told her, a room for himself and another for the secretary. A bath and dressing room. Convenience for preparing a simple meal.

"Bedroom?" enquired Oggie, jotting all this down on a pad.

"Naturally. I can't put up at the club for more than a few weeks."

She pressed a bell four times; it was some sort of a code ring. A gaunt young woman with greenish-blonde hair presented herself; recognising her from Oggie's parties, Ginever said hello. She smiled reservedly.

"Get me Miss Guevara, will you? Put the call through here.— You know Guevara?" Ignoring his gesture of refusal, she refilled his glass.

"Painter, or something, wasn't she?"

"Did Virginia's portrait. Vee always hated it. I don't know where it is; she's probably slashed it. I went to Paris," said Oggie gruffly, "and when I came back all her stuff was cleared out. Left a note she'd put it in store. After nine years—it gives one a jolt. Guevara's going to Mexico," she interrupted herself. "Her place might suit you, until you've found something permanent."

She was giving him some details when the secretary came back; there was no reply from Miss Guevara's number.

"All right. Go on ringing. Wait a minute; put down the address and the number for Mr. Ginever.— Where are you lunching?" she asked him. He told her, at the Caprice.

"I'll ring you there if we manage to contact Guevara."

"It's kind of you to take the trouble, Oggie."

148

"I might be asking you to take trouble for me, one of these days!" she glinted at him.

Just before the secretary reached it, the door opened, and his wife walked into the room.

"Darling one—"

She caught sight of George—who switched his head away—and the air shook.

"Hello," said Oggie.

"Well—!" said Blythe, and laughed. Her fur hat and the shoulders of her mink coat were flaked with snow; the soles of her ankle-length seal boots were caked with the impure, brownish snow of the streets. She was followed by Oggie's maid, who carried a pair of satin slippers, received the coat and the hat, and offered her shoulder for Blythe's support as the latter kicked off the boots. She ran her fingers through her ruffled hair; it was no exaggeration, thought Ginever, to say that she preened herself.

"Well: what are *you* doing here?" The note of amusement was admirable; neither under- nor over-stressed. Oggie, who had turned her back, silently filled a glass and offered it to Blythe, who rejected it.

"You know I don't take champagne in the morning!"

Oggie spoke levelly.

"George and I have been having a chat."

"Oh?" Blythe sat suddenly on the edge of a chair, ducked her head, groped for her handbag, found a looking glass and powder, dabbed at her nostrils and round the quivering line of her mouth. "I seem to have come in at the wrong moment! Sorry about that—see you later," she muttered, and, getting up as abruptly as she had sat down, made for the door, which Ginever reached ahead of her.

"It's all right, I'm going. There's just one favour I'd like to ask the pair of you. Be so kind as not to use my house for the next week or so." (It only occurred to him later, that it was the first time he had ever spoken of the house as "his.") "Not till Flavia's gone away. Afterwards—it's all yours."

Oggie nodded a curt assent. He did not get the door closed in time to cut out Blythe's shrill utterance:

"What have you been saying?"

—and Oggie's retort:

"Oh, shut up, you little . . ." The epithet she applied to his wife happened not to be in Ginever's vocabulary, although he was familiar with it. He did not care for its application to Blythe, but at the same time was forced to admit that it fitted her perfectly.

He had an unsatisfactory interview with his accountants: that is to say, more unsatisfactory than usual. The senior partner was away; a younger member of the firm, whom he had met only once before, managed, under a veneer of bonhomie, to make him sound and feel a fool. The session with Oggie, and its upshot, had deprived him of such meagre powers of concentration as were his. When at last he descended into the brief gully of Vigo Street, he knew he could not face luncheon at the Caprice. He walked round the corner into a Cork Street gallery where he had bought a picture or two. There was nobody there, for the moment: only Lavinia, lifting her lovely, stylized head, directing towards him the startled glance of her immense eyes, breaking into her sudden smile that carried a sweetness of pepper trees and mimosa. Her hello was light as a feather. It carried no reminder of their brief attachment, which had come to nothing because Lavinia, just then, was getting over a much more serious attachment, wasn't ready, was too scared to expose herself to another affair which would involve her in emotional upheavals and lead to nothing. "Kind, kind and gentle was she." He did not even have to pretend interest in the current show. He gave a perfunctory glance round the walls, to be polite; it was all modern, Middle European stuff. She didn't like it any more than he did, but it was her business to sell it. He enquired about a small Italian oil, a woman's head, to which he had taken a fancy before going to America.

"My little Florentine lady?— I'm afraid she's gone. Just before Christmas. She's been around so long, she felt like my own, and I put her down in my office. As a matter of fact, you were so keen about her that I thought I'd keep her until you came back."

"Who bought her?" Not having given the little picture— "school of Fra Angelico"—a thought, from that day to this, he was faintly affronted. Luce would have liked it. Galleries did not like giving away the names of their customers, but he and Lavinia had shared a proprietary affection for the fifteenth-century panel, which she had picked up in an auction "because she could not resist it," although she was unlikely to sell it; the gallery dealt mainly in the moderns.

"Virginia Harrison came in with a friend—I can't remember the friend's name. I gave them tea downstairs and they both went crazy over the picture. Virginia insisted on buying it, and I couldn't say it wasn't for sale, though it wasn't in the exhibition. You know what they are, she and Oggie—they'd been rather tiresome, buying and then un-buying! But this friend wanted that picture and Virginia wrote the cheque out there, on my desk, and they went off with our little lady tucked under their arm!— It's rather sad, isn't it?" concluded Lavinia.

"Yes, I'd like to have bought it."

"I didn't mean that. I meant, about Virginia and Oggie Schneider. Or haven't you had time yet to catch up with the talk of the town? They're both such nice people. There always seems to be a special sort of sadness about the break-up of that sort of household.— Where are you lunching?" she asked inconsequently.

"Where'd you like to lunch?"

She laughed.

"I've got a dinner party tonight, so I've got some sand-

151

wiches. Come down and have a drink. You look," she added, "as if you could use it."

"I've got to ring the Caprice."

"Well, can we do it for you?"

His head was spinning— "I'm supposed to be lunching with Bill Littlejohn. Say—I'm detained; and I'll ring him tonight."

He was stumbling down a narrow stair, and falling into an armchair in Lavinia's office. A glass, in Lavinia's strong, dark hand, appeared at his elbow.

"Drink up, and be quiet for a bit. I'm going to eat my lunch."

She was sitting opposite to him, serenely smiling and smoking a cigarette, when he came out of the short, dead sleep into which he had fallen.

"Hello! Like some coffee?" Moving gently and slowly, she filled a cup and brought it to his side. He mumbled an apology.

"I expect you've been hitting it up since you came back. How's Blythe? And Fla? It's ages since I've seen Fla—I bet she's grown into a beauty."

"How old were you when you knew about Lesbian relationships?"

Her eyes widened at him. She let out a bubble of laughter.

"You're not serious."

"I'm asking you."

"We went to boarding school. Some of us had crushes on the teaching staff, and some of them had crushes on us. Jealousies and hysterics, that wore off. I suppose you could call it a sort of baby Lesbianism; we'd never heard the word. It didn't make any impression. When we left school and started to have boy friends we felt rather sheepish about our crushes on Miss This or Miss That. Little brutes, we were. There was an arts Mistress who was mad about me; when I met Ruan I just brushed her off. Guilty? No, of course I didn't feel guilty; there was no 'guilt' in those burning embraces we exchanged on the dark landing outside the dormitory. I don't think it ever occurred to us that there was anything 'evil' in it; only 'silly.'

"When Ruan and I got married, Dawn came to the wedding. Dawn! Can you imagine a more ghastly name? And I didn't know, then, that she was christened Dora. There was rather a miserable little scene when she insisted on coming up and helping me to change for the going away. It came over me, suddenly, that she had prepared me for just that very thing: getting married. Not meaning to, of course."

"Hello," said Ann, walking into the room. "I say, I could hear you sneezing downstairs." She was carrying a glass with two bubbling tablets in it. He took it from her meekly. "You look as if you've got a temperature; head aching?"

He nodded, glancing at the note pad in her other hand.

"What have you got there?"

"Just two calls; one's from Long Island—"

He put the glass down carefully, not looking at Ann.

"Mrs. van Thal will be here the day after tomorrow—"

"That's good," he heard himself saying fatuously. So the crying of his heart had reached her! He felt himself tremulous and dissolving with love and relief; the edge of the desk under his hand was swaying gently up and down.

"She's air-mailing the details—she was very sorry to miss you, and she said not to ring her until you get the letter.— The other call was from Mrs. Schneider; she's been trying to get you at the Caprice."

"Oh, yes, I cut that lunch."

"Have you had any food?" demanded Ann sternly.

"What did Mrs. Schneider want?" he sidetracked her.

"She's got you a studio at Primrose Hill. I was just going up to have a look at it, if you hadn't got anything special for me. Look, George, I'm going to get you an egg; 'feed a cold—'"

"Where's Fla?" he interrupted. Her brow crumpled.

153

"In bed. She wouldn't have any lunch and I must say she looks pretty ghastly."

"Well, have you had the doctor?"

"That's just another of those things." She smiled palely. "He's down with flu and the locum's run off his feet; he said he would come in tonight. However, I've taken her temperature and it's normal. I'm inclined to agree with Blythe—that it's another of her Lausanne-dodging tricks. But she really does look awful, poor kid! She calls it a 'chill' and says she only wants to be let alone."

"How long have you known about this Schneider set-up?"

Ann crimsoned; she was obviously very much taken aback.

"Let's get a few things straight, shall we. I want Blythe to divorce me, but I've got to make sure Fla's all right. Well, she very much isn't all right. What has been going on here while I've been away?"

"I don't think that's a fair question," she was beginning, when he checked her.

"I'm not concerned with 'fairness' at the moment. I want to know what's turned my daughter from a normal, healthy kid into a little psychopath."

"Well, as you obviously know, what's the point in asking me?" fenced Ann.

"I'm asking you: did my wife and Oggie Schneider conduct their affair right under Flavia's nose?"

"You're exaggerating," said Ann, after a silence. "I don't think you know how simple Blythe is. From the minute she got caught up in this—this infatuation, so far as she was concerned we were all stone-blind, stone-deaf, and half-witted. I think that irritated Mrs. Schneider. They had rows—"

"In Flavia's hearing?"

"In the hearing of the whole Square, I should think," said Ann dryly. "And then there was reconciliation, and crying—"

"Don't tell me Oggie lowered herself to tears!"

"No, of course she didn't. I've got a lot of respect for her;

154

she's a fine woman. But—poor Blythe! I had to be sorry for her, though I was often mad with her for her lack of self-control."

"And Fla?"

Ann shrugged.

"I think she'd got the situation summed up even before I did. And she would have taken it in her stride, if it had not been Blythe, whom she used to adore. I think," said Ann carefully, "it started with simple jealousy, and grew rather quickly into something more complicated.

"I think," she said, "if Blythe had started an affair with a man, Fla would have accepted it with some degree of philosophy: would have taken for granted that you'd divorce and probably had some anxiety for her own future. That's the common pattern with kids nowadays. But this went outside the boundaries of her own experience and her imagination and she got in a panic."

"There's just something I don't get," said Ginever, as she paused. "Wouldn't it seem reasonable, in the circumstances, for Fla to be glad to get away from home?"

"It would," agreed Ann, "except that she's seeing everything at the moment as a 'plot' against her. Fla's a natural fighter, and she's all out to thwart the two people who, in her estimation, have behaved badly, to her—and to you."

"So all that political and sociological stuff was just so much boloney."

"No, not at all," Ann corrected him. "She's absolutely sincere about her Nuclear Disarmament and Colour Bar and all that—but her antagonism to Blythe is on top for the present. She's 'in standing water': half a baby, half a sophisticated adult. She feels alone in the universe—long before she's prepared to accept aloneness. She puts on a terrific act of toughness, but she hasn't got the toughness of those kids she calls her 'gang.' She needs you badly," concluded Ann.

"She's not given any sign of it, so far. She's done nothing but dodge me since I came back."

"That's bluff—and fright. She doesn't know whose side you are on—hers or Blythe's. She feels involved in all this business, and she's torn between her loyalties. She adores both of you, but she's hating Blythe just now—you know, honestly I'm sorry for Blythe! I'm sorry for anybody so incredibly stupid. She's as devoted to Fla as you are, and she doesn't even faintly connect Fla's outrageous behaviour, her rudeness and unkindness, with her own conduct. She doesn't see that Fla's resistance to attempts at discipline aren't just pure bloody-mindedness, but resentment of what Fla calls hypocrisy. She's simply got her head in a bag—and she isn't even happy about it! Whatever pleasure she gets out of Mrs. Schneider's company is killed stone-dead by Fla's attitude—which, God help her, she can't understand!— Well, George, I'm terribly sorry you've come back into such a mess; it won't do any good to your work."

"You don't know the ha'f of it!" he said, in a mock American accent. "I came back to ask Blythe for a divorce."

"Well, that would seem to be the solution," said Ann, having taken this in. "If she's inclined to divorce you."

"And there," said Ginever, "you have it. She isn't."

"My God," said Ann. "You *are* in a jam."

"Whatever's happened here," he said, "is essentially my fault. You know that." Ann had been in on all his entanglements and dealt with them coolly, with perfect tact. "I've been no good to Blythe and I've got no grounds for complaint if she's found her own compensation. But I've got to look after Fla."

Chapter Ten

Flavia's face, peony crimson, looked out of a tangle of untidy bedclothes. The TV was on; Ginever walked across and switched it off.

"Oh, Daddy; I wanted to watch—"

"Sorry, honey. Mind if I smoke a pipe?"

There was a pause before she tittered.

"'Course not; I mean—why ask?"

"Sign of advancing years—on your part and mine. It's not considered 'the thing,' to smoke a pipe in a lady's bedroom."

She wriggled resentfully.

"Don't be so silly.— Of course I'm all right," she answered his question. "I just felt like stopping in bed. Why they have to make such a fuss!— Did you want something, Daddy?" she asked, impatiently. "Sit down—if you like," she added; it was not to be interpreted as an enthusiastic invitation, but Ginever let himself drop into the armchair and struck a match, averting his eyes from the disorder of the room. "Well?" snapped Flavia.

"Do you remember—'If you would fall into any extreme—'?" He poked the stem of his pipe to the printed words over the head of the bed. She was visibly startled.

"'Let it be on the side of gentleness,'" he concluded. "So I've come to ask for your gentleness."

"I don't understand," she faltered.

"A lot of things have gone wrong since I've been away—it's all right," he checked her smothered exclamation. "I know all about it, and we don't have to discuss. Some things are better unspoken." He caught her outflung hand; the small fevered palm shrivelled in his. "'Let it be on the side of gentleness.' That's a doctrine of love, isn't it? And love is something to be honoured, whatever form it takes, whatever changes it may undergo." He sounded to himself like a preacher.

"Would you mind," said Flavia bitterly, "talking to me as if I were an intelligent person?"

"Would you mind," he retorted, "not setting yourself up in judgment on something you know nothing whatever about?

"Whatever's gone wrong is my fault; get that into your head. Your mother and I have agreed we don't get on; that's been going on for a long time, but we've done our best to keep it to ourselves, on your account."

"Do you suppose I didn't know? Daddy—really! I can understand this ostrich performance from Mummy," she said scornfully, "but not from you. Do you think I didn't know about Marda Lane, and Lady Urcott, and the rest of your girl friends?" she stunned him by enquiring. "Anyhow, what's all the fuss about divorcing? I've been expecting it for years," she shrugged.

"And what would you have felt like, if—?"

"I don't know." She shivered slightly. "I'd have taken it, of course," said Flavia loftily. "We all do. There are more important things . . . So what's happening?"

"I've found somebody I can get on with, and so has your mother."

"But, Daddy—"

"Don't let's have any 'but Daddy' for the present. We're trying to plan out our lives the best way we can, for ourselves and for you."

"You can't expect me to live with my mother and Oggie Schneider!" She sounded hysterical.

"Fla, look: we haven't had time to think anything out. Nothing whatever will be done without your agreement." She was obviously looking on herself as a victim.

"To what am I supposed to agree? To living with Mummy and Oggie?— I used quite to like Oggie, until she and Mummy came back from New York. She's always been nice to me—and fun—and we've got on. And then—all of a sudden —it was different. They made me feel I was in the way. There were rows when I went out and rows when I stopped in and had my friends. What for? I ask you—what for? *They* didn't want me. They were always in the drawing room, or Mummy's bedroom. One night I went down to say goodnight, and the bedroom door was locked. I knocked. I could hear their voices, but the light wasn't on; you know you can see the slit under the door. I called Mummy, and she didn't answer. They stopped talking. I felt scared.

"I'd read it all: Oscar Wilde and Claudine and the *Chansons de Bilitis*—"

"Where did you get hold of Bilitis?"

"In Sandra's shop. She gets quite a few books, and we giggle over them. You made me learn good French," she reminded him. "Colette's my favourite author. Somebody popped in an old Claudine—*En Ménage*—I'd never read it before. There were a lot of words I didn't know, but I understood most of it. And everything dropped into place—like the last bits of a jigsaw." She caught her lip in her teeth and thumped the bed. "And I didn't like it. I don't like it! I don't know why; I never minded much about your girl friends—in fact, I was quite fond of Marda—but this is different. It gives me a funny feeling. It's all very interesting, and all that, reading about these things, but—you understand, don't you?"

"Quite; it's very entertaining to read a Maigret, but not so

159

good to find a corpse on your own staircase.— I'm sorry, honey."

"*You* don't have to be sorry about anything. I'm sorry for you, Daddy," she said, with a touching assumption of maturity; then with a lapse—"But what's going to happen to me?— Oh"—she clapped her hands to her mouth—"I think I'm going to be sick. Please leave me alone!" Before he could intercept her she flashed out of bed and into the bathroom, slamming the door in his face.

He met Blythe on the stairs.

"Oh. I was coming up to see Fla. Is she better?"

He shrugged; she glanced up at him with an impatient little noise.

"What is it this time? Hysterics?— Poor little girl; I wish—I wish—"

"It's a bit late for wishing," he said dryly, and politely indicated that he wanted to pass. "Well, the doctor's coming tonight.— You haven't forgotten," she reminded him, "that we've got the Heslops for dinner? He wants to run a couple of articles about you—"

"Oh God; those—!"

"I thought you liked the Heslops."

"Is that why you asked them?"

"You know, George"—she turned round on him—"I think you'd better see the doctor, when he comes in for Fla. Everybody's having flu. You look to me—"

"Never mind how I look." He followed her down to the drawing room and closed the door behind them. It seemed as if their previous conversation had gone for nothing. "What particular axe are you grinding tonight?" he asked, not ill-humouredly.

"I do take exception to that!" said Blythe, looking beautiful, as she always did when she was indignant. "You know perfectly well that my axe-grinding, as you call it, is for your benefit."

"Have you ever heard of over-sharpening a blade, so it loses its cutting edge?"

"Poor old blade. So do I ring the Heslops and say you're 'indisposed'?"

"Leave it, leave it."

"You know, George," said Blythe, in a painstakingly reasonable voice, "you'll have to pay some *practical* attention to the future. Will Lucy—"

"Shut up about 'Lucy'!" he shouted rudely.

"All right; I was only wondering if she was prepared to support you while you're turning out your masterpiece."

"Do you know," said Ginever, "I'd no idea you hated me so much."

"Th—that's not hate," said Blythe, stammering a little.

"Then why throw in my teeth that—?"

She said with one of her disconcerting, her almost shocking bursts of candour:

"I suppose it's jealousy. Since we were married, I've given you all I had in me. It wasn't much—anyhow, it wasn't enough. I've realised that a long time. I tried to make up in other ways. It hasn't been a success—from your point of view, or from mine. We both wanted something the other couldn't supply. My pride was involved. I suppose you would admit I've been useful—" She checked his exclamation with a gesture.

"Then comes along this Lucy. And—I'm not being sarcastic —I just hope she'll be as useful as I've been . . . I mean that, sincerely."

"Thank you. I think all this adds up to is the sooner we're apart, the better for everybody. Jealousy is as foolish on your part as it would be on mine. And—while we're on it—I'm moving out in a day or two."

"Where to?" she asked in astonishment.

"I may have got a studio," he said vaguely. "You've heard about it, from Oggie, anyhow—I'll shift into an hotel for a few weeks."

"But is that necessary? You've got all your tackle here. Surely you'll have enough peace and quiet when Fla and I've gone!"

He could have reminded her that peace and quiet did not depend wholly on solitude.

"No, I think, as we've made up our minds to the break, the cleaner we make it the better. To tell you the truth"—he decided to match her candour with his own—"I'm afraid it's going to be absolutely impossible to work here. I'll get my tackle, as you call it, shifted while you're away—"

"A nice job for Ann that's going to be! You know we made that store-place for you downstairs."

"I'll probably leave that, if it doesn't inconvenience you, until I've had time to make some plans."

"Oh—please don't strike attitudes," she said impatiently. "How could it inconvenience me?— But could I remind you that when two people have shared a house for sixteen years, they can't float away in separate directions without a certain amount of co-operation?"

"Fair enough; I'm prepared to co-operate."

"Especially not where other people are concerned. Could I remind you"—it seemed to be her new, favourite expression—"that we've got a daughter?"

"By God," he said quietly, "that comes well from you! Do you think," said Ginever, "there's much to be gained, at this moment, by going into all that? On one point, I imagine, we're in accord: that Fla mustn't suffer any more than we can help for our discordancies."

It was one of Blythe's best dinners; she had taken endless trouble, and her genius for entertainment came out in the simple menu, the table decoration, the dress she had chosen, the atmosphere she created. Beside the Heslops, she had invited a BBC pundit with his latest (and most attractive) wife. Blythe was the perfect hostess.

The Heslops were an entertaining couple, in great demand on social occasions; to secure them for a party was considered a feather in your cap. If you rated socially, or were in the news, there would be a mention in Andrew's column. They were too busy to accept invitations that did not carry some kind of kudos. Agneta ran a question-and-answer page on antiques in one of the women's glossies; what she knew about antiques could be put in a thimble and covered with a strawberry leaf, but she was in with the dealers. They ran a travel page in one of the Sunday papers, and were always flashing off to the latest continental resorts; brilliant journalists, they had, in effect, created resorts. They had, in effect, done more to ruin charming and secluded islands and beaches and villages round the Mediterranean, Adriatic, and Aegean coasts than any of their contemporaries; it paid off in a big way, in a much-photographed house in "Little Venice," off the Regent's Canal (Agneta had coined the name, but, in one of her rare moments of forgetfulness, had omitted to patent it; so others got the credit) and a no less publicized "contemporary" country house in Sheffield Park.

Andrew and Agneta were basically nice people; there was no doubt about it. They were careerists, and their careers lay essentially in publicity. They would probably love to make friends with simple, insignificant people, but life was too short. It was worth while, to accept a dinner invitation from the Ginevers; otherwise they would not have been there. Otherwise Agneta would have rung Blythe up—"Darling, it's too poisonous: Andrew's got this thing with the X's" (the Y's or the Z's). "Can we come in later for a cup of coffee?" It happened to suit them, to confirm their acceptance of Blythe's invitation: George was just back from New York and might have some entertaining chatter.

163

And the BBC couple; he was very Third Programme and esoteric. She was a pretty young thing, vaguely connected with Talks. Recently married—she was his third or fourth wife—their preoccupation with each other was a little embarrassing. However—they also were just back from New York.

"I hope you saw the play?"—from Blythe.

Third Programme batted his eyelids.

"Which play would that be? We saw a few—"

"Oh, *Baz!*— Mrs. Ginever means her husband's play. I'm terribly afraid we didn't; we were only there a few days," apologised his wife.

"Actually, we were running to schedule"—with a small, moustached, and bearded smile. "We didn't make a special effort, because we heard it was coming to London. That's right—I hope?"

Admiring his skill in fielding the ball, Ginever said the plans weren't yet cut and dried.

"Actually, we're waiting for the Webbs," flashed Blythe, and, with a barbed glance at Ginever, dared him to contradict her.

"The Webbs?"—Agneta Heslop, with a sceptical lift of the the eyebrows. "Didn't somebody say they were going in to a Tennessee Williams?"

"We've got our fingers crossed!"—from Blythe. "Leo isn't very keen on his part, but Cath's mad on hers. So of course we can't tie it up until something comes through from their agents."

"Who's your second string?"—from Agneta: calling Blythe's bluff. Ginever caught her eye: trust the Heslops—!

"Now, Aggie!"—Blythe, over-sprightly.

"I mean, you'd have to keep the American slant, wouldn't you, George?" Agneta appealed to him. "I think that's why so many American shows flop when they come over here; it's not just a matter of pace—as a lot of people make out; it's an

164

ideology. Now you can't put an English actress into Cath's part! It simply wouldn't make sense."

"Darling," purred Blythe, "you haven't seen the show, have you?"

"Yes, as a matter of fact we have," said Heslop unexpectedly. "Ag and I were over in November—wasn't it?" He consulted his wife. "And we had a drink one night with Bill Littlejohn; he said you were planning to bring it over here. A nice job of work; it ought to go—though, of course, if you don't get the Webbs, the casting will be tricky. You'll have to get an American for that part—what's it—Aurelia."

"Do you remember that awfully striking girl we met at Bill's party? We both thought she'd be a wonderful Aurelia: quite different from Cath, but—why, she was a friend of yours, George; Lucilla—Lucinda—some odd name. Wasn't she understudying?"

"We've got nobody particularly in view and no theatre—so far," said Ginever heavily. "The play—it's more Pete Marrotti's than mine—wasn't much of a hit; the Webbs kept it afloat. One or two people over here seem to be interested— dimly—" It pleased him to play it down, against Blythe's resentment. A sound offer had come through, that morning, from Harry Lasker, and he had not told Blythe; what more concern was it—any of it—of hers? If the play came on—if— he would have something to set against his overdraft.

They had reached dessert when the Scandinavian girl came in.

"It is the doctor, to see Flavia."

"All right, Ingrid. Sorry about this," said Blythe, rising and dropping her napkin on the chair. "Fla's got a cold, or something. I shan't be long. George—?"

They trooped up to the drawing room, where there were coffee and liqueurs. There was an imperceptible relaxation. The little Talks girl started to talk, quite spontaneously, about Spain, where apparently they had spent their honeymoon.

165

The Heslops knew Spain—superficially: the new resorts between Málaga and Gibraltar. Somebody mentioned Toledo; Huesca came up, and the seventeenth century of literary and artistic renaissance under Lastanosa. And so—Gracián. He dodged the subject of Gracián, on which the BBC man was prepared to enlarge—if they had been alone, they might have got on to it—and swung the conversation to a discussion on which writers in English had most ably translated the Spanish mystique. "Hemingway!" cried the Heslops. The names of Bates and Brenan came up; somebody recalled Kate O'Brien, somebody else Pritchett. Agneta Heslop laid down as an axiom that only Catholics could write with authority about Spain, and Heslop winked at Ginever; according to Agneta—a recent convert—"only Catholics" had the answer to mysteries which had disturbed the human race over centuries. Well, she could be right; but it seemed a pity to spoil the discussion by dragging in religion. He filled the glasses again. The BBC man—his name was Lightfoot—turned out to be extremely well informed about Toledo and the Visigoths; about the *Criticón* and the contemporary poets who coloured the early works of Gracián. Lightfoot dropped all this out, through his waxen face and little black beard; Ginever who, to begin with, had not liked him, felt that quickening of sympathy which almost inevitably takes place between individuals linked by a mutual interest. He was reminded of Walton, and the long Edinburgh nights when they pored over the translation.

Andrew and Agneta, chipping into the conversation from time to time—his geography was better than hers—appeared to be considering how Toledo could be made into a "resort"; that, thought Ginever, with some degree of satisfaction, would defeat them. He made a mental note to keep in touch with the Lightfoots, and had just got up to give her a light for her cigarette when the door opened and Blythe came in. He saw at once that something was wrong.

"Sorry to be such a long time."

Agneta went over to her and, with one of those intimate gestures a certain type of woman employs to her woman friends, delicately flicked a trace of powder from the collar of her gown. Blythe drew back as if she did not like it and looked at herself in the glass; yes, she had put on too much powder.

"Everything all right, darling?" asked Agneta brightly.

"Oh yes—Fla's got a chill, that's all; thank goodness it's not flu. Is there any coffee left?"

"It will be cold by now," said Ginever; it was nearly an hour since she had gone upstairs. He moved towards the bell, but she stopped him.

"No, it doesn't matter—unless anyone else would like some more?" Pleasantly as she spoke, her entrance had broken up the mood of their conversation, which now became bright and gossipy, led by Andrew and Agneta; they had the hides of their profession, those two! Surely, he thought, a look at Blythe's face would suggest tactful withdrawal; then he saw that Mary Lightfoot had got it. She said something to her husband and they both got up at once. Blythe said the usual perfunctory things of the hostess, and, as they reached the door, Lightfoot turned to the Heslops.

"Not to break up the party—but if you'd like a lift?"

Ginever found himself liking Lightfoot very much indeed. Even Agneta could not remain impervious to so plain a hint, enforced by Mary Lightfoot's nod towards the clock.

"Goodness," said Agneta, "it's never—! Darlings, the evening's simply galloped!"—not the happiest of observations, as her hostess had been absent a large part of the time. The women went across to Blythe's bedroom to collect their wraps. Heslop took the opportunity of saying to Ginever:

"I'll ring you tomorrow, old boy"—meaningfully; to which Ginever, automatically using a formula he detested, replied:

"All right, old boy. But—ah—I've got rather a thick day; mind if I ring you?"—a job he could delegate to Ann, having warned her that nothing on earth would induce him to contribute to Andrew's "profiles."

Lightfoot was saying:

"If you're thinking of covering that stretch of the country, I've got a few maps that might be of use to you." Ginever discovered that the little "beardy" smile, which to begin with he had thought precious, was very pleasant. Lightfoot said, almost shyly, "Cartography's a bit of a hobby of mine." He added, as they shook hands, "And good luck to the book!"

"What's this? A Spanish book?" Trust Heslop to have his nose to the trail.

As Ginever went poker-faced, Lightfoot said airily:

"Only an arrow shot into the air; it might fall to earth—say —in Huesca? Come round some time and see my maps."

Luce would like the Lightfoots. As he was conducting his guests down the stairs, Ginever heard as clearly as though the words had been spoken aloud, in Heslop's voice to Agneta: "Did you hear that one?— Ginever's off on a Spanish book." And Agneta: "Oh God! Can't somebody tell him Spain's old hat?"

He expected on his return to the drawing room to find that Blythe had gone to bed. She was crouched on the hearthrug, over the remains of the fire.

"Well—what's the doctor got to say about Fla?"

She laughed shortly, and stretched up her hand.

"Give me a cigarette. She's just announced she's pregnant!"

"Is she?" he heard himself saying.

"Of course she isn't!"

"But what made her think—?"

"She didn't! We've just had a real show-down," said Blythe grimly. "I'm glad, in a way, it was this young chap, not Dr. Meachard; he was perfectly cold-blooded about it."

"Goddammit—about what?"

"I made him examine her, there and then. Our daughter,

you may like to know, is *not* a virgin! But, so far, there are no results."

"Well, that's a mercy anyhow—poor kid." He paused. "I'll go up and see her."

"Save yourself the trouble. She's asleep by now, with two pills inside her. So far as I'm concerned," said Blythe, "it's over to you. You can hardly make a bigger mess of it than I have!"

"True enough," he hardened himself to say.

"But Fla's my child, and I *love* her!" she insisted.

"That goes for me. The trouble seems to be, we haven't loved enough."

"Speak for yourself! Ever since she was born, I've given my whole life up to Flavia. But—but one can't go on like that," she stammered. "Everybody's got a right to a life of his own! You took your life—"

"Yes, yes. I let you down," he said heavily.

"We've let each other down; was that your fault or mine?" she said, with a sudden gentleness that took him aback. "If we've got to talk about faults, 'the fault is in our stars.' My parents were old; I was brought up in a school of thought that was old-fashioned, even before the war—the school that obliged a girl in my position to get married. Until I met you—I never wanted to get married."

"Did you then?"— From this midnight mood of confidence, what truths might emerge, what mysteries be resolved?

"Not really. Before I met you, I had been in love with two women."

"How much in love?"

"Obsessively," said Blythe, after consideration. "Maria and I never kissed, never touched; but I thought of nobody else. It was so pure a thing"—her voice broke a little—"I could almost cry to think of it. I don't expect you to understand that!"

"Don't you? Then why tell me?" he said, with gentleness. "And the other?"

Her beautiful face hardened.

"That was something different. She was old enough to be my mother, and married. Happily. I liked him—quite. I was her 'flirt'! My, my; what she put me through. That was when I met you. Just then she'd found another girl: much prettier and more—more sexy than I. So I made up my mind," ended Blythe on a whisper, "to pay her out."

"My—God," said George Ginever.

"Go on; hate me all you like. This is—isn't it what the Spanish call 'the moment of truth'? After living a lie for sixteen years, there's something in getting back to the truth!"

Then why, he marvelled inwardly, won't you let go of me?

"Now, let's get back to Fla; she's got to have a home, hasn't she?"

"She's got a home; with me."

"And Oggie Schneider?"

"I don't know what you two were talking about the other day," said Blythe icily. "I'm not proposing, at present, to set up house with Oggie. I'm very fond of her, and she's very fond of me; I don't see any reason for publicising the fact. She and Virginia made themselves the talk of the town—"

"Oh, nonsense; it's customary, in civilised society, to take Lesbian households for granted."

"I don't think it's an advantage, for a girl of Flavia's age, to grow up against the background of a Lesbian household."

"For God's sake, take your head out of the bag! Flavia's aware of the relationship between you and Oggie. Whether you choose to conduct it honestly, or in some rather sordid, backstairs fashion, can't make any difference to her. The damage is done, so far as Fla's concerned, and I've only got one thing to say. If you won't divorce me decently," said Ginever, "I'll take it to the courts, and it'll be a hell of a picturesque case. It'll make the gutter-press happy for a week. I don't even know if it's possible to get a divorce on Lesbianism, but I'll be seeing Maurice Cohen.— By the way, I'm going to Glasgow tomorrow—that's to say," he corrected himself by a glance at the clock, "today. Something I signed up for last year; Ann reminded me. They're worth talking to, up there. And Luce is arriving the day after," he concluded flatly.

"You'll be back for that," said Blythe, without emotion.

"Naturally. And I'd like Fla to meet her."

"Why—if one might ask?"

"I don't want her—Fla—to feel she's shut out of our confidence. I don't want her to build up a false picture of my relationship with Luce, or to feel doubtful of her own position in relation to us."

"I object! I really do object," said Blythe violently, "to your introducing Fla to your mistresses!"

"There's no need to pluralise it," said Ginever dryly. "And, if it comes to that, have you got much room for objection?"

Chapter Eleven

Before leaving the house he went to Flavia's room, tapping
very softly, in case she were asleep. The darkly shaded lamp
beside the bed avoided her face, which was turned away. She
gave no sign, but he guessed she was pretending. He touched
the hair scattered on her pillow, and wondered if he imagined
a stiffening of face and body. He said, just above a whisper,
"See you tomorrow—baby"—the name he had not given her
for years; he could even remember the birthday when she announced, "I'm not 'baby'! I'm Flavia Ginever," and occasions
when he slipped up and made some sort of a comic apology
which she accepted with a small, dignified frown. He looked
now for the soft pucker between her delicate brows, but remembered that Fla was now too old to mind being called
"baby." He looked down at the small, precious face, drained—
deliberately?—of expression, and decided Fla was foxing. So
he did not trouble to lower his voice. "Just bear in mind—will
you?—that I love you." He did not trouble to close the door
quietly behind him.

He came face to face with Blythe, dressed to go out.

"Do you have to bang around, when the child's supposed
to be resting?" she accused him.

"I guess I've not disturbed her.— Well, I'll ring you when
I get back."

173

"Oh yes. Of course. You'll be spending the day with Lucy," said Blythe negligently. "Give her my regards. I'll expect you when I see you."

He gave the worst lecture he had ever given in his life. He listened, with a half-stunned incredulity, to the flat, mechanical sentences dropping like bits of lead on an unreceptive audience. Glasgow audiences had always been among his favourites; all Northern audiences were worth while, but Glasgow most of any. He liked them and they liked him. They gave each other of their best. At least, that was how it had been. Now he felt a build-up of antagonism between himself and one-time friends who felt he was letting them down.

The discussion which was supposed to follow the lecture was limited to a few indifferent questions, which he answered tersely. There were some stiff courtesies with the chairman and the secretary—"So when can we look out for the next book, Mr. Ginever?"—and he was on the train which, if it ran to schedule, would get him to Euston in time to bathe, shave, and be at the airport to meet Luce. He did not sleep. Against the rumble of the train his mind was a confusion of Luce, Luce, Luce, and the book he wanted to write, and would never write, and would he ever write anything again, and, if he did not, what sort of a future had he to offer to Luce? . . . Suppose I'm written out? What happens to us then? Journalism: a highly specialised branch of the profession. It was only worth while if you pulled down one of the plum jobs, or got yourself an impressive name as a free-lance. Such journalism as had come his way arose from his position as a novelist, as Harry Lasker had been kind enough to point out. As a high-up novelist, you could command a variegated public which would read your articles for the sake of your books. But for a writer of his age and experience successfully to conduct the swing-over from fiction and literary criticism to full-time journalism would be to pass a miracle, the elements of which were not

174

within George Ginever. Know thine own limitations! A tap dancer wasn't supposed to lead the corps de ballet, or an operatic singer to make a success in pop. George Ginever, author of *The Grey Goose Is Gone*, etc., etc., etc., could command a reasonable respect from editors so long as he remained in the best-seller lists; but was unlikely to be taken seriously by those who could pick and choose from the shining galaxy of young men down from the universities with their built-in assurance, their classless opinions, their cultivated cynicism . . . Was I like that, twenty years ago? No, satire hadn't come in, and fiction writing wasn't a build-up of gimmicks, and the youth-cult had not started—well, not noticeably. You still showed some degree of becoming respect to grey-beards in their forties; it was not taken for granted that the adolescent mind was in every way superior to that of experience—sharper and more advised.

Look out, he apostrophised himself. Disgruntlement gets you nowhere. And what have you got to be disgruntled about, anyhow? *Tu l'as voulu.*

He got a bedroom at the Euston Hotel and looked at himself in the glass, wincing at the reflection. After shaving in the bath he plunged his face into cold water and rubbed and patted until it looked rather more human. He tipped the remains of his flask into the black coffee, when it came up, glanced at his watch, and rang Ann at her flat. There was at first no answer, and he was about to ring off when she came on the line, rather breathlessly.

"Sorry—I'd just got to the lift."

"I thought you'd be having a lie-in. What do you want to be out so early for?"

"Taking Pavlova for a hair-do." Pavlova was Ann's poodle. "Well, how did it go?"

"Lousily. Look: I won't be in this morning. How was Fla last night?"

"She was having dinner in bed when I left, but she seemed better, and—and ordinary. Can we get you somewhere later on?" asked Ann. It occurred to him that she was being a little over-casual.

"Is Fla all right—really?"

"I guess she'd like you to give her a ring—when you've got time."

"Now?"

"It's a bit early, if she's had one of her pills. How about lunch-time?"

"I'll ring. Give her my love, and say I'll ring."

On the way to the airport a breakdown-truck towing a tractor had slewed itself across one of the roundabouts and there was a half-mile queue that road repairs reduced to a single line of traffic. He was sweating and swearing before they pulled up at the channel. The flight had just been posted. He leapt up the stairs to the observation deck, just in time to see the big, silver insect advancing up the tarmac, swinging into place—and then they were running the gangways up, people started to stream down, and he ground his gloved palms into his eyes which were misted with the cold and drove his sight towards the human tangle at the foot of the gangway, trying in vain to find her. His heart thudded; she was not there—not anywhere among the crowd that was being herded towards the bus. She wasn't there—it couldn't be true—then she was there, last of all, leisurely, lingering on the stairs. He let out a yell and flung up both his arms. From that distance she could not see or hear. Then he was banging on the barrier outside the Customs, and the passengers were drifting in with maddening slowness, looking for friends and waving to them, and at last—at last!—she was there, all of her longness and thinness disguised in a long tweed coat, her face thin and grey and concentrated—until she suddenly caught sight of him, and her hand flashed up, and it was as if a star blazed between

176

her upturned collar and the shallow, down-turned brim of her hat.

"Oh—oh; it's worse than I imagined. It's just terrible. To love anyone so much, to love anyone so, so much! It is real, isn't it?"— They were in the Daimler. "I mean," stammered Luce, "we don't have to wake up?

"I've been dreaming this—just this—don't take your hand away—for nights on end. I daredn't go to sleep in the plane for fear of waking up and finding it was only another dream. So I started imagining: you wouldn't be here to meet me, or you'd be different—or something—"

"Well?"

"Well what?"

"Am I different?"

"Oh, darling—no—yes—I mean more so— Stop me talking for God's sake—I'm being hysterical, I'm making a fool of myself—"

"I like you that way. I like you any way."

"Can we have a drink somewhere? I think I'd be fine if I could have a drink."

They stopped and he ordered Scotch. She refused his suggestion of another.

"Not till I've had something to eat. I couldn't face breakfast. Now I'm going to be sensible.— Oh, darling, you're so beautiful. You look rather ill, though"—touching the thin skin under his eyes. "Nothing the matter, is there?" she asked anxiously.

"Nothing—now you're here. Like you, I could do with some food and some sleep."

"Why do bags under the eyes suit men and look revolting on women? I love your elderly, battered look. So what's the matter?" persisted Luce, and cut short his protestation with, "Does Blythe know I'm here?"

"I told her you were coming. She sent her regards."

"Damned civilised of her." Her lips split over her beautiful,

177

broad grin. "So let's all be civilised. So give her a kick in the pants for me. Tell her what to do with her regards. Oh, that was good!" She puffed out a breath of relief. "Hartington Green—he sent you his love by the way—Hartington says that if people would be common, downright common once in a while, half the psychiatrists would go out of business. He's been trying to put that idea over on Belle-mère for the last few years, but it doesn't take; she still pinches her lips when I say 'dam'.'" She dropped her head on his shoulder. "So Blythe isn't playing?"

"We'll work on to that presently, shall we? Did I mention I love you?"

"It's funny," said Luce, brushing this aside. "When I met Blythe—you know, in the hospital—I almost liked her. Maybe that's putting it too strongly. I admired her. I'm given to admiring my own sex; we're so dam' marvellous, the acts we put on! And of course I wasn't involved—then. I thought she was rather a gorgeous bitch. I suppose I hated her—as Belle-mère would say—*au fond*— Don't interrupt: I've got to say something now, quick, because it's going to cover this little time we've got together. Whatever Blythe does, or won't do, I belong to you. If we can't get married—I don't understand the workings of your English laws—that's okay by me. Okay, darling?"

The Daimler pulled up in Arlington Street.

"But it's—it's—goodness, it's not—last time I was here was when Carola and I were kids: one of Dad's business trips to Europe," she was saying incoherently.

"It's as good a pub as any."

"But we—I—I'm not staying here!" stammered Luce; he had got her key from the reception and was seeing her and her modest suitcase into the lift.

"Don't be longer than you can help. I'll be waiting right here."

"But, George Ginever, you're crazy . . . !"

178

When she rejoined him her lipstick was brighter and her crisp and shining hair just brushed the ice-white neckline of her tweed dress that matched the travelling coat. She had the thin, immaculate elegance which seems to belong exclusively to American women, gloves, shoes, and handbag of matching crocodile—and two little furrows driven in between her dark, delicate brows.

"Darling—this is quite crazy. Or have you won the lottery or something? Who do you think I am—Jackie Kennedy, or something?" she was protesting in an undertone, as he steered her towards a corner table. He ordered, got rid of the waiters, and covered her hand with his own; they were early and the restaurant still nearly empty.

"Have they given you a good room?"

"Room! Somebody's made a mistake: I've got a suite, on the park."

"All right; we'll have coffee up there presently. It wasn't so easy, finding an hotel. I tried one or two"—he did not add that there were others he could have tried, but did not wish to take Luce where he had been in other company. "Anyhow—it's a party."

They kept up the pretence of eating through the soup and the smoked salmon; when the lamb cutlets arrived he caught her eye and she shook her head.

"I thought I was hungry, but—"

The waiter asked if they would care for something else, and Ginever said No and asked for the bill, which he signed, and said to send up coffee and brandy to Mrs. van Thal's suite. They went up in the lift, and stood at the window, looking across the rain-shrouded, sleet-shrouded park. Luce whispered:

"I can't believe any of it. Is this you? Is this me?"

The tray with the Cona and the china and glasses was brought in and set down by the fire. The dusk gathered in.

He awoke before she did and stretched his hand cautiously towards the bed table on which he had left his watch. Gently as he had moved, her eyes opened; her long bare arm dropped like a warm serpent across his throat. She asked sleepily: "What's the matter?"

"Nothing. I've just remembered I've got to make a call. Go back to sleep, honey; I'll take it in the other room."

"I'm wide awake," said Luce. "What's the time?"

"Going for six."

"D'you mean we've wasted all this time—just sleeping?"

"D'you call it waste?" His hand lingered on her shoulder, slid down her ribs to rest on her hip, slipped lower down and was clipped into the warm dampness of her thighs. She laughed quietly and stretched out, soft and luxurious; turned over on her belly, thin and beautiful and nude.

"I'm so happy."

"Me too."

"We haven't talked about anything. It doesn't matter, does it? I don't seem to care about anything in the world. Put in your call, honey, while I run a bath. What are we going to do tonight?"

"What do you want to do?"

"Whatever you say."

"All right; we'll have dinner up here, shall we?"

"That would be blissful."

"I'm just going to call Fla."

"Does she know about us?" asked Luce.

"Not explicitly. No details."

"That's right; no details. When am I going to meet Fla?"

"Soon. She's been a bit sick."

Luce sat up, clutching the quilt about her naked shoulders. "How sick?"

"I'll tell you later." He reached over for the pack of cigarettes, lit a couple, and gave one to her.

"I want to get it over—meeting Fla. It's going to mean such a lot, to both of us."

"I know."

"I wondered—could we have lunch someplace? Or is she too sick?"

"I'll find out—now."

"I'm dreadfully nervous."

"You don't have to be. Look, there's a place I eat sometimes in Knightsbridge; it's—it used to be one of her favourites. I'll tell her to meet us there at one o'clock."

"That's fine.— Darling, do you think—could you manage to be a little late—so Fla and I would have time to get—to get used to each other—?"

"I'll leave you to yourselves altogether, if you like."

"No, no; that's too tricky. If anything went wrong it could be very uncomfortable for Fla."

"How do you mean—'if anything went wrong'?" He frowned. "What could go wrong?"

"Almost anything." She gave him her kind, comfortable smile. "She loves you; that's one thing. So we've got to play it easy. Don't make a fuss over me, honey."

"I've got a lot to tell you about Fla—"

"Keep it. Let's start out even, knowing nothing about each other," interrupted Luce; brushed his hair with her lips and, wearing the guilt like a toga, went through to the bathroom and closed the door.

He started to get dressed, moving drowsily, quietly, contentedly; lit another cigarette and looked through narrowed eyelids and the smoke at his image in the glass. He caressed his jaw and remembered his shaving pack was in the overnight case he had left in the cloakroom; luckily his beard was not perceptible for half a day. He dallied over his tie, decided for the present against his vest, and elbowed into his coat; strolled into the sitting room and switched on the lamps. Stood for a moment at the window, watching the lights of taxis shuttling along Piccadilly. It amused him to reflect that Oggie Schneider, within a stone's throw, might be looking out on the same scene—possibly with Blythe at her shoulder!

He picked up the receiver, was about to dial the house, changed his mind, and rang down instead for the evening papers: then to the restaurant for the menu.

When Luce came in, sleek and well-groomed, he dropped his feet from the sofa and dropped the newspaper—guiltily. When he kissed her she smelt of Roman hyacinth—his favourite scent.

"Well?"

"I've just been looking at the new books; Fullerton's taken a pasting—I can't think why. He sent me the proofs—bloody good. But they've got a new chap on the column—"

"Fla—?" she questioned.

"I'll ring now.— My love. My dear." He held her closely. Her eyes met his steadily. "I wanted," he said incoherently, "everything to stay just as it was: you, me, and nobody else in the world."

She lifted his hand and laid her lips to it briefly; picked up the receiver and handed it to him. As she was turning away he caught her wrist and pinned it to his side, holding her there while he dialled the number with his forefinger.

The bell had only rung a couple of times when Blythe's voice came tautly on the line.

"Yes?"

"Hallo." Before he could add anything she was screaming at him.

"Where on earth have you been? We've been ringing you everywhere."

"Sorry. What's the matter?"

"Fla. She's gone."

"What do you mean—'gone'?"

"Just that. I went to her room—and there was a letter on the bed, addressed to you. Marked 'Private,' and sealed. If you're not back in a quarter of an hour I'm going to open it."

"Don't do that. I'm coming."

Luce's face floated towards him.

"You heard."

"Yes." Her hand gripped his.

"I'll ring you."

"All right. Don't worry about me. I'll be here."

"I've ordered dinner up here; don't wait."

"I can look after myself."

"If I don't get back—"

"I can still look after myself. Hurry, darling; Blythe's in a state."

Going down in the lift, he told himself: I expected this. Not *this*, not Fla. But it was too good. Something had to happen. Life did not resolve itself as easily as all that.

Luce by herself in that big, opulent suite—intolerable thought. All the things they ought to have been saying to each other—swallowed up in that folly of sleep! Dearest, I haven't told you about . . . and about . . . How long are you here for? I don't even know that. For Christ's sake, Luce, don't go until we have been together: really together—not only our flesh but our minds you said belong to me no matter what did you mean it of course you meant it but do you realize . . .

The taxi stopped. He got out and pushed the key in the lock.

"Hey, mister; am I to wait?"

Wait?— Of course; he had forgotten to pay. He left the open door, shoved a ten-shilling note in the driver's hand—and Blythe was on the stairs.

Chapter Twelve

The letter started without affectionate preamble.

I've thought it over and come to the conclusion that the best I can do is get out of the way. I'm only complicating things for you both. I know you and Mother are going to break it up and I'm the problem. I hate that so I'm clearing out.

Here are the details so there's no mystery or any of the stuff that makes headlines.

My address: 4 Lindale Road, Newhaven. There's no telephone. N.B. I'm calling myself Flavia *Green*—I've got to stick to the initials because of my suitcase and things. Bull is down there and says he can get me a job. I think it's in a cafe but will let you know. I will be sixteen next month and we plan to get married. Of course I'll have to have your permission because of my age.

Please don't stop us getting married. It won't last, but what does? We depend on each other a good deal. I don't know how to put it without being beastly, but it's easier to depend on somebody of your own age. You see through the same glasses. You've got the same values, and you don't have to take time off explaining or excusing yourself.

As you know, quite a lot of people of our age are living

together, but I've thought it over and I'd prefer to be married, even if it comes unstuck in a year or two. Bull and I have had some rows about it, he says I'm a square and perhaps I am about just that one thing, but I think he will come round. It's funny, he's nineteen but in some ways I'm older than he is. I've had a good home and quite a fair amount of freedom, considering. Bull's parents have been rather stupid and repressive so he lives in a state of permanent rebellion for which I don't consider he's to blame, but he could easily go delinquent which of course is silly and unnecessary and I might be able to help him a bit. Anyhow plenty of girls are marrying at sixteen now so whatever objections you and Mummy think up, *please* don't base them on my age. And you won't do anything silly like making me a ward of court or whatever it is, will you? I do trust you not to do that.

I don't know how it's going to work out, but we'll manage somehow.

It's taken me nearly all night to write this, and I haven't said any of the things I meant to. Too difficult.

I hope you will both be very happy, though I sometimes think happiness is one of the hardest things to achieve today, in spite of Welfare State, etc. Or because of. But easier for your generation than mine.

Give my love to Grans and Ann.

N.B. If you think of coming down here please send a letter or a telegram first.

N.B. I am old enough to know my own mind and it is quite made up to this.

Your loving daughter.

He passed the sheets of paper silently to Blythe, who read them. Her drooping hair hid her face, but he knew that she was weeping. Presently he put his arm round her; she made no resistance but, dropping her head against her shoulder, continued to weep. It was so long since he had held her like that—relaxed, helpless—that he felt extraordinarily moved. She muttered something.

"What do you say?"—with his lips against her hair.

"My fault . . . all my fault . . ."

"Never mind about 'faults.'"

She jerked herself away, keeping her head averted, and did things with her handkerchief.

"Well—what are we going to do?"

"I don't know. Perhaps send a telegram."

"I'm going straight down—now."

"Don't do that," he said quietly. He picked up a pad, scribbled a line on it, and passed it to her. "'We love you dearly.' That's enough, isn't it, for now?"

"Don't be absurd! We've got to get to her—"

"Why? What good will that do?—Wait while I send this." The operator repeated the address and the message primly.

"Thanks," he said, and hung up. He stood for a moment with his back to the shaken woman, then with deliberate calm crossed the room and took a cigarette out of the box on the mantelpiece; lit it slowly and let a couple of whiffs of smoke out on the charged air. "Now: suppose you tell me what's happened while I've been away."

The doctor had come in, and appeared to be quite satisfied with Flavia.

"That was in the morning, just after you left. He said we'd better keep her in bed—but she flatly refused. She even talked about going out! I put my foot down on that," said Blythe.

So they had rather a sulky luncheon, and afterwards Fla said she had "things" to do, and went up to her room.

"It was pretty plain she didn't want to be left alone with me. I thought for a while about going up and—and trying to talk. But she might have locked her door, and I couldn't beg her to let me in; I couldn't!"

"So—?"

"So about five o'clock I sent Ann up to ask if she wanted some tea. Ann came down and said she was lying on her bed, watching TV, and didn't seem to mind about tea. So I did a tray and took it up myself . . ."

"Didn't Ann say I don't want tea?"

"I wanted a cup myself and thought you might change your mind. Do you feel better, darling?" said Blythe, trying to keep her voice calm and ordinary.

"What do you want, Mummy?" asked Flavia coldly.

"Do you have to speak to me like that? It hurts very much," said Blythe, in a strangulated voice.

"So I'm the only person who's got to be hurt?"

"Oh, Fla . . ."

"I don't want any talk!" The child's voice was shrill. "It's all happened—and there's nothing more to say—so far as I'm concerned. Except— No, no; I can't say it."

"We used to say everything to each other."

"Did we? That was a very long time ago."

"But—but, my little girl—I love you."

"Do you? Do you—after what you did to me the other night? The doctor—that horrible, shaming performance—"

"Fla! Pull yourself together. You brought it on yourself, with that silly lie, my darling—"

"Oh, don't say 'my darling' like that, Mummy! Oggie Schneider's your 'darling'!"

"You are being very foolish," said Blythe, pulling herself together. "You are my daughter, my little girl—and about —about that business with Dr. Mills: will you tell me what you'd have done in my place?"

"I don't know what you mean."

"You put up that cock-and-bull yarn about being pregnant."

188

"It could have been true," muttered Flavia.

"It could, but it wasn't, and you knew it wasn't. Didn't I have to call your bluff for everybody's sake?"

"Will you tell me exactly what you'd have done about it, if I hadn't been bluffing?"

Blythe shrugged her shoulders.

"I don't think that will lead to a very profitable discussion. — Fla: you're so intelligent—how did you imagine you would ever get away with it?"

"I don't think," she whispered, after a silence. "I stopped to imagine. I—I lost my head."

Blythe waited until her own voice was steady.

"How very, very unhappy you must have been. I ought to have known." She swallowed. "Will you—will you try to forgive me?"

"Oh yes," said Flavia; and added confusedly, "people can't help being the way they are. I don't believe we'd ever understand each other—not in a hundred years. But there's no reason for us to quarrel, is there? Quarrelling's terribly adolescent. You call me your 'child,' and 'little girl.' But you overlook one thing: that I'm your daughter, and my Father's —so I'm not exactly simple. The sort of education I've been given doesn't make for simplicity, either. Parents these days seem to want to have it both ways; we're brought up to use our brains, encouraged to form our own judgments and develop interests pre-war kids knew nothing about. Then, when the treatment takes, we're slapped back and reminded we're 'only children'! So we're driven into rather—rather exaggerated attitudes in defence of our own principles."

"You aren't going to Lausanne," interrupted Blythe. Flavia gave her a wintry smile.

"I'm afraid I've taken that for granted."

"Can't you tell me what you want—really? Would you like," pursued Blythe, "in two or three years' time, to try for one of the colleges? Have you got any sort of notion what you want to make of your life?"

The child shook her head slowly.

"You know I haven't got the brains ever to make the University. Even if I wanted to. But I don't. I don't want that sort of specialised life. If I'd like anything, it would be to write—like Daddy. But to write you've got to get experience—"

"Yes, my dear heart. But, to make the best of what you call experience, surely you've got to have some sort of educational grounding? You're only fifteen; there's time to spare."

"Is there?"

"Fla, there's no point in brooding about the atom bomb. It may come; it may not. But we can't regulate our lives on an assumption of imminent destruction."

"No, Mummy, of course not." She spoke with patience. "I don't think anybody does, if they've got sense. I don't expect to die in some sort of a Hiroshima; I'm not frightened of the idea. But we're in a sort of—what's the word?—*limbo*, aren't we? What we're struggling against is dehumanization. Science and mechanisation—that's what a lot of us are scared of. We don't admit it, of course; we're 'children of the age.' The rock-and-rollers; the good-time kids! That's the way you think of us—don't you? Oh, I don't mean it personally; you and Daddy and me.

"The values—the virtues," she went on confusedly, "the things one reads about in history books: they're still there; they can't die. But nobody's got time to tell us about them— at least, in schools. We've got to rediscover them for ourselves. We have to do it secretly, privately, among ourselves— covering up with pop and all that, because we're scared of being laughed at." She caught her breath and flushed crimson. "Sorry—to be a bore," she muttered.

"Do you think—I'm ever bored?"

Flavia laughed.

"Of course. Well—do you mind if we say goodnight now?"

"Goodnight? What about your supper?"

"If Ingrid would like to bring me some soup."

"You won't come down?"

"No. I don't think so. Thanks, Mummy."

"It's not much fun—having dinner alone."

"Well, you don't have to, do you?" said Flavia pointedly.

Blythe got up. There was nothing to be gained by pursuing the conversation on these lines. A blind had lifted quickly, and as sharply been let down. Perhaps, tomorrow . . .

"Wouldn't you like an omelette?"

"No, thanks; just a bit of soup."

"Well, then—goodnight." She bent to kiss Flavia who ducked her head quickly and presented the parting of her hair to her mother's lips.

"Goodnight."

"Wouldn't you like your bed made?— And the room straightened? It's in rather a mess."

"I *like* my room in a mess," said Flavia fretfully. "That's the way I keep it. Don't fuss, Mummy. It is my room, isn't it?"

"I only want you to be comfortable."

"I am very comfortable indeed, thank you," said the child, in a stately voice. As a concession, she added, "I might have a bath, later on, I'm all right; there's nothing to fuss about!"

"You've got your sleeping pills."

"Oh yes; for crying out loud! I shan't want one tonight."

Why can't I take you in my arms? Why can't I break down this icy curtain? Why should I be afraid of offending you, Fla? Why can't I find the right words, the right gestures . . . I'm your mother, Flavia.

As she passed the study she heard the tapping of Ann's typewriter. She hesitated; should she go in? Some proud, spiritual withdrawal held her back. She was not in the mood to meet the calm, knowledgeable assurance of Ann's grey eyes; always understanding, always kindly—what business had Ann

191

to understand, or to be kind? All the proud secrecy in Blythe's nature rose in an unreasonable antagonism to one who, over the years, had proved herself not only a good servant, but a good friend to them all. Ann, with her detestable quiet tact, knew too much. Unobtrusive, apparently incurious, she had involved herself in their private lives. No; she could not, in this moment, turn to Ann for sympathy.

There was one lamp on in the drawing room; the room was too quiet, too tidy. The evening papers were there, the fire banked up with logs, the furniture in order. An awful, empty tidiness. She paced for a while between the window and the fireplace. Put on some more lights. Call Ann? *No.* Ann would soon come in, without being called. "Do you want anything before I go?" "No, I don't think so. Have a drink." "No, thanks. How's Fla?" "She's all right. She just wants some soup." "Shall I take it up before I go?" "No—it's early, isn't it?" "Yes; I've finished—for once. But I'll stop on, if you like." "No, there's no need. I'll cope."

After this imaginary conversation, Blythe picked up the receiver and dialled.

"Hello, sweet."

"Hello." She knew her voice was tight and unnatural. She choked out the words, "I'm afraid I can't come round to-night."

"What's the matter?"

"Fla. We've had a bit of bother."

A pause; then—

"All right; I'll be right round."

"No, don't. I've got to look after the child and then—and then I'm going to bed. I'll ring you in the morning."

"Where's George?"

"You know—up in Glasgow. He's coming back tomorrow."

"I'm coming round now."

"Oggie: don't—please."

"I'll be round in ten minutes"—and the line was briskly

cut. The receiver was still in her hand when the door opened and Ann came in, dressed for outdoors, with her despatch case under her arm.

"Sorry. I only came for the letters."

"Oh—I haven't got any. Are—are you going?"— An idiotic observation.

"Unless you want anything?"

"No, no. Won't you have a drink?" she said desperately.

"No, thanks very much." She glanced at her watch. "I'm afraid I'm late, I'm only just going to catch the post."

"Are—are you having dinner anywhere?"

"Well—as a matter of fact"—Ann looked surprised—"for once I've got a date. A real, tarting-up date!" She laughed. "These things always come along when your decent frock is at the cleaner's." There was a silence. I can't go down on my knees and beg her to cut her date and have dinner here with me, thought Blythe. Her hands were trembling. "Are you all right, Blythe?" said Ann's voice behind her.

"Of course.— Well, see you in the morning."

"Unless you want anything, I'll be rather late; George said he wouldn't be in before lunch. I want to take my pood to her coiffeur. Is that okay by you?"

"Of course it is.— Did—did you mean that about your frock? Would you like me to lend you something?"

"No—bless you! Sure you're all right?" insisted Ann.

"Don't be silly; of course I'm all right."

"You look rather washed-up.— Fla's better, isn't she?"

"You've seen her?"

"I went up to say goodnight. She was on the telephone, so I didn't stop. The bath was running, so I guess she's going to have a tub and settle down. Wonder what sort of a time George is having in Glasgow," said Ann, disconnectedly. "Well—à demain."

"Have fun."

193

With the quiet closing of the front door behind Ann, it was as if the last of her defences had gone.

"I'll have my dinner on a tray in the drawing room. Flavia will have some soup and *croûtons,*" she said to the servant on the stairs.

"It's my night out."

"All right, Ingrid; I'll take it up myself. Tell Mrs. Roberts to do my tray as soon as she likes." They were on the landing; the door-bell purred.

"No," said Flavia, on the telephone. "I've got a cold; I'm not coming out. How's Sandra? All right; say I'll be round to see her sometime—sometime tomorrow."

She got into the hot bath, squeezed the sponge over her shoulders and her head; let her hair float like seaweed on the water; closed her eyes. I'll get dressed, and go down and have dinner with Mummy. We can't go on like this. She *is* my mother. Oh, damn, yes—she's my mother!

"I asked you not to come," Blythe was saying weakly. Oggie was stripping off her overcoat, dropping it on the floor, lighting a cigarette. She puffed two or three times before speaking. In her tailored suit she was like a little stout gentleman; a big diamond flashed from the little finger of her left hand; her right was thrust into the pocket of her slacks. She might have been a man straddling the hearthrug of his club.

"What's all this about keeping me out?" she said gruffly. Blythe let her head fall back against the sofa pillow and her eyes close. Perhaps, she thought, she was going to faint. Her lips moved.

"I didn't mean—I'm rather upset—"

"So I'm not wanted when you're 'upset'? That's a new one, isn't it?"

"Don't let's have a scene."

Oggie gave a satirical honk.

"Me—make a scene? *Tu te trompes, chérie!* 'Scenes' are not my *métier.* I am perhaps allowed to enquire what you're 'upset' about? Now"—she cleared her throat, tossed the butt of the cigarette in the fire, and sat down on the end of the sofa; her small, firm hand lay on Blythe's knee. "What's it all about?"

"Fla—I can't bear—"

Oggie waited.

"You can't bear—?" She listened with patience to a flood of incoherencies. "All right—I think I understand. It must be hellish, not to have the courage of one's own convictions.— I'll have to think this over, you know. I've buggered up my life pretty considerably, on account of you. I was very fond of Virginia, you know, and she of me."

"Then why don't you go back to her?"

"The simple solution? Ha! That's what you want, is it? You *slithy* little tove. You cheap collector of sensations: of wifehood, motherhood, and—and whatever you could get on the side, in the way of emotional kicks. Faithful to nothing, except your stinking little ambition to be Mrs. George Ginever. Poor old George," concluded Oggie with her short laugh.

"So—really—you hate me?"

"I wish to God I did," said Oggie, in a low voice.

"You despise me," insisted Blythe.

"No, I'm not given to despising anybody—except myself." She shook her head and stood up abruptly. "Well, that's enough for now. You've had your ration!"

"I don't know what you mean."

"Don't you? All right, I'll tell you. You don't really care about anybody, excepting yourself. I've known that for quite a while. You don't know what it means," said Oggie roughly, "to love a person, and accept what loving means, of pain and sacrifice. So you've mucked up your life with your husband, and your life with your daughter. You've had a hell of a kick, haven't you, out of this affair with me; I've

195

given you a whole new range of emotional experience. I don't grudge what I've given, but—"

She picked up her coat and started to shoulder herself into it. Blythe's arms went out blindly. There was silence, then a smothered exclamation. The familiar, overwhelming scent, the pressure, the inevitable yielding . . . Oh my darling my darling . . .

"Mummy."

They leapt apart. The child stood there in the open door, the light of the landing behind her. She had put on the ruby frock; her small ivory face was slashed with the lipstick that matched the frock.

Oggie was the first to recover herself, moving instinctively between Flavia and Blythe.

"Hello, Fla; are you all right now?"

Flavia's eyes went speechlessly from one to the other. Blythe was on her feet, sweeping back her ruffled hair.

"Darling. Come to the fire. Dinner's coming up in a moment: I'll tell Mrs. Roberts—"

Flavia said in a voice that was like the tinkling of glass, "Sorry I gate-crashed. I only came down to say goodnight—Mother. Goodnight—Mrs. Schneider." She closed the door quietly, with dignity, behind her.

"Dam' all," said Oggie, and picked up her coat again.

"So then what?" asked Ginever.

"She'd got dressed—she'd taken the trouble to get dressed and come down to dinner with me. Mrs. Roberts brought my tray, and I sent her up to tell Fla it was ready. Her door was locked, and she said she didn't want anything; she'd gone to bed.

"I didn't see her until lunch-time. I'd got—oh, I don't know: a hen party. Fla came down, and behaved beautifully; so far as I was concerned, she could have been a casual acquaintance. She said she didn't want coffee, and went upstairs.

About three o'clock there was a ring for her; I took it—one of her friends. Ann was doing some letters with me; I asked her to call up to Fla. There wasn't any answer. She went up, and a minute later called down to me. There was a mess of clothes—and that letter, addressed to you, on the bed. It was Ann who noticed—who discovered—that one of her suitcases, the big new one we'd bought for Lausanne, was gone. Ann said you'd promised to ring up sometime. You might at least have done that!"

"I know. I meant to."

"So we've been ringing everywhere we could think of. So now: what are we to do now?"

He said, after reflection:

"Nothing for the moment. What should one do? She's left a perfectly explicit account of herself. She's got plenty of common-sense; she's all right for now."

"'All right?' A child of fifteen? You can do as you please; I'm going to take the next train from Victoria—"

"Will you sit down for a minute and let's work out a few sensible ideas?"

"I'm afraid I don't feel sensible about my daughter's running away from home."

"There's no need to dramatise it. In a technical sense, she hasn't, as you put it, run away. As she herself points out, she's made no mysteries; all things considered, she's written a mature letter. The last bit"—he turned the page over—"suggests that she's quite prepared to see us; by implication, to talk things over."

"I can't see much point in talking!"

"Well, you don't propose to put the law on her, do you?"

"What's the law for," she blundered, "if it doesn't protect children like Fla from their own follies? I take it you don't propose to give your blessing to this—this ridiculous proposition? Can't you see that the first thing we've got to do is get her home—"

"By what means? Kidnapping?"

She glared at him.

"No, I'm not being funny. I've got too much respect for Fla to make jokes. But, short of legal intervention or kidnapping—how exactly do you propose to get her 'home'? What, at the moment, have we to offer her in the way of 'home'?

"I think that's what we've got to consider, both of us, before crashing in on Fla with all the weight of parental authority behind us."

"And meanwhile let her go on living with the Dawlish boy?"

"Why not? She's slept with him already. That's a secondary consideration. They both know they can't get married without our permission.— Let's think it over and discuss it in the morning."

"Discuss what?" asked Blythe dully.

"Our own future. Can't you see that's the answer, so far as Fla's concerned? At any rate, it gives her a choice."

"Oh—that old divorce . . ."

"Go to bed and take one of your sleeping pills," he said gently; he was very sorry for her.

"Do you think anything would make me sleep tonight?— Don't go, George," she begged him. "Don't leave me all by myself!"

And Luce—all by herself?

"We've got to talk about things," she was saying incoherently. "What time is it?— Good life, Mrs. Roberts will have gone. I told her to leave me something on the hot plate. Come on; one must eat!"

"All right," he said, after a silence. "I'll be down in a few minutes."

"Of course," said Blythe. "You'll have to telephone Lucy. Say—I'm sorry to spoil your evening."

Chapter Thirteen

"Everything's perfectly all right," said Luce's steady voice. "I've had dinner; thank you, darling, it was lovely. Now listen: I've found the address of a girl who was with us in one of the summer theatres. I rang her up a few minutes ago, and she's given me an address in Bayswater; it sounds quite nice. So I'm moving out tomorrow morning. So you don't have to bother about anything—see? Here's the address, and the telephone number. If you've got time, ring me in the morning. If you can't, don't worry; I understand."

"There's a pub on Queensway." He gave the name. "Do you think you could find it? We could have lunch there."

"That would be fine. But you mightn't be able to make it. Let's leave it—and you give me a ring."

"I'll be there—come hell or high water. My dearest. You know you're my dearest?"

"Oh yes. That's why it's easy—for me."

She had got there first, and got a table in an alcove. The waiter took his coat; he let himself drop beside her. Her thin hand slid warmly into his.

"It's nice here. I like your London pubs."

"Well—she's come across. Blythe. She's going to divorce me."

She gave his hand a light squeeze.

"We'll save that for later. Tell me about Fla."

"There's her letter."

"Well, honey, what have you done about it?" Having read it slowly, she gave it back to him.

"I've wired and written her. I expressed the letter, but I doubt she'll have it before tomorrow morning."

"You're not going down to this place—what's it?—"

"No, not immediately. Why? Do you think I ought to?"

"No," she said, after reflection. "I think it's better for everybody to wait a little. Does Blythe agree?"

"Look." He rubbed his hands over his face. "We talked until half past five this morning. Half fighting, half being terribly nice to each other! I suppose we dredged up all the muck of the last ten years. We said some pretty ugly things to each other.— I think," he said, signalling a waiter, "I'd feel better if I had a drink."

"It's my lunch," said Luce quickly. "Two double Scotch—"

"On the rocks?" grinned the waiter.

"Two double Scotch," she repeated, ignoring the impertinence. "And steaks—rare; with sauté potatoes, and tomay—tomatoes, grilled."

"What's this?—our wedding breakfast?" he grinned; his head was spinning with fatigue.

"Go on, darling. Tell me more."

"All right. I love you."

"Sure. That's being obvious."

"Well—when we've finished eating, I've got a surprise for you."

"I like it," said Luce, with her elbows on the window-sill of the studio. She leaned out and snuffed the winter air—less clammy than the cold within; the electric stoves he had switched on had not yet taken hold of the damp, deserted iciness that fogged glasses and laid mist on neglected surfaces.

He looked with distaste at the smoke-blackened curtains, stained and dingy upholstery, and the unpleasant litter its late occupant had left behind her. The dirt and the squalor.

"I like it," she repeated, and flung her arms around him. "Why do you look like that? What's the matter?"

"I didn't know it was as bad as this. I wouldn't have brought you," he muttered.

"It's going to be marvellous! Oh, George Ginever, haven't you got any imagination?" She rocked him in her arms. "You leave this to me! You leave it to me!" She looked round possessively. "It's going to take a while to dry out and clean up; I guess this Guevara girl was a slut! It ought to be habitable in a few days' time—"

The telephone burred.

"Hello. Oh—hello, Ann. Yes?— What?"

"Blythe's just gone. She asked me to let you know."

"Gone—where?"

"Down to Boar's Hill. She said she might be back, but she's taken an over-night case. She hates night driving—I shouldn't think she'll make it. There've been some calls—no, nothing from Fla. Harry, of course. Bill Littlejohn; he got in on the morning plane. He says to ring him at the Savoy."

"What for?"

"The play. The Webbs are coming over. He wants to talk to you about the set-up.— Look, George: I'm holding the fort, just in case Fla should ring."

"I've given her this number.— All right; I'll be down."

With Luce pottering gently in the background, he rang Harry Lasker.

"All right, all right," he interrupted the latter's blasphemy. "Tell Bill I'll be there in an hour. And you'd better be there, Harry, to hold the coats! What? Of course I'm going to do the bloody play. Listen: that second scene in the second act wants re-writing, every line of it, for our theatre. What? To hell with Pete: whose idea was the play, anyhow? The whole of that act was wrong: I'm telling you. Oh, sod off, Harry—I'll be seeing you."

About half past nine there was a ring from Lady Adela.

"George? Goodness, how hearty you sound!— Yes, Blythe's here, having hysterics all over us—very trying! We haven't got much sense out of her so far, but I gather you're divorcing? *Most* sensible, my dear; you must both have had a very trying time. There's some muddle about Flavia— I can't hear very well, something's gone wrong with my 'aid.' Never mind; we all send love. Are you there? Send me Fla's address in Lausanne, will you? Blythe's too, too vague! I'd like to send the child a line of welcome. Sorry, dear, I can't hear a word. We must have lunch one day and talk it all over. . . ."

And ten minutes afterwards, another ring.

"Daddy?"

He made himself say calmly, "Yes, chicken?"

"Oh—I thought it might be Mummy."

"Where are you?"

"In a call box at Victoria."

"All right; I'm coming."

"No, don't; I've got a taxi waiting."

"All right; I'll be seeing you."

Her tired, untidy head was against his shoulder.

"I've made a real fool of myself."

"We all do, from time to time."

"He bolted—we had the most awful row—and he bolted. He didn't want me," said Flavia loudly, with pitiful bravado.

"Did you want him?"

"I only wanted—somebody," she stammered. "Being by yourself—what happens—what happens, Daddy? If you and my mother are divorcing, what happens to me?"

He held her close.

"Don't you trust me?"

"Yes, of course."

"Well, then, I love you. Your happiness is bound up with mine. Come on; sit down, and let's talk."